TIME OCULAR

By Joe Wolfe

Library of Congress Control Number: 2004113514

ISBN 1-932701-44-3

Originally published September 2004

Contents

Acknowledgements

Thanks to the following who have inspired this work.
To God and His unconditional ever-present Love,
To Judy Hall and Judy Rosenthal for their encouragement.
For the message of Forgiveness as taught in
A Course in Miracles
For
Dr. David R. Hawkins author *of Power vs. Force*
Gary R. Renard author of *The Disappearance of the Universe*
To Linda McNabb, author *of One Again*
Neale Donald Walsch for his original *Conversations With God*
Marrianne Williamson
Eckart Tolle, author of *The New Earth*
Joel S. Goldsmith, author *of A Parenthese In Eternity*
Carrie Triffet, author of *Long Time No See*
To Jay McCormick for his on going
contribution of loving presence,
To Reverend Margo Ruark of
The Peace Center in Berwyn, Illinois and her gracious hosting of
the largest ACIM group gathering in the Chicago area,
And to my dear friend,
Rick Lovell D.C. whose tireless motivation keeps me active

Time Ocular

"It's a machine that when operated correctly, can actually see into the past," Luke explained.

"It enables us to view whatever went on, in high resolution, every detail of every event that ever happened, as if it were going on right now!"

~~~~~~~~~~~~~~~~~~~~~~~~~~~~~~~~~~~

Chapter One

Five hundred miles south of the area known as Giza , near a river at a point called Tura, was the dock port where thousands of years ago, sixty ton granite blocks were unloaded and transported to the site of the building of the Great Pyramids.

Heavily freighted barges moved the rock north to locations where, now thousands of years later, current archeological excavations went on and where, as never before, archeologists stumbled upon one of the greatest finds of all time.

A team of diggers worked diligently as Samiha Salaha, a native scientist sat cross-legged at a high point over looking the activity, as her workers brushed away centuries of sediment from a recently discovered burial find.

Born in what was then known as Palestine and educated in the United States , she loved her work. She loved her helpers and encouraged them well with free food and generous wages.
This day was particularly hotter than most. A backhoe lumbered noisily in the distance, as it moved slowly toward a foreman who waved his arms wildly and screamed out instructions to the operator.

Suddenly, the big, cumbersome machine struck an unseen object in the ground and vaulted into a dive. The sand and dirt beneath it had given way to a soft area causing the machine to loose control.

It bucked violently, as the driver struggled desperately to regain his hold in check.
Samiha sprang to her feet and looked out onto the scene. The driver displayed a determined grimace and he urged the machine to move forward, while its metal tracks screeched in response, spinning to the limits of its capabilities.

Then a large area of the soft earth gave way and for a moment it appeared as if the powerful dozer would loose the battle and sink. Samiha shouted for help as she sprinted closer. Teams of her helpers quickly responded, dropping their tools and they ran to assist.

Then, as abruptly as it had begun, the backhoe struck yet another object and stopped. The operator was stunned as he looked down at the tracks in confused dismay.

The machine had settled upon a long, artificial rock formation that appeared to extend well into earth. By then Samiha had reached it.

"Get down out of there!" she ordered him.

Joseph, her engineer and project manager had stayed with her all the way, running along behind her at the first sign of trouble.

The driver of the backhoe scrambled out of his cockpit and clamored on his knees across the tank tracks and dropped safely at the feet of his employers.

"I am so sorry," he apologized.

Samiha dismissed him with a wave of her hand as she peered down into the top of an ancient masonry wall that had been revealed by the dozer. The machine had rested atop the newly unearthed wall structure, long ago buried and sealed by many centuries of weather and sand. Samiha's engineer approached it carefully and fell to his knees. He ran his hands along its smooth surface then looked up at Samiha with an expression of disbelief. She too, was mesmerized by the find.

"Get everyone here!" she commanded.

Many weeks of painstaking excavation went on. Careful attention was paid to maintaining an undisturbed monument of this kind, by scores of workers who worked long hours each day meticulously brushing away ages of sand and dirt. Eventually it was realized, that what they had stumbled upon was a small ancient town. It was a town that had been constructed by the

ruling powers of the time that would serve as a place of residence to house the many people that had been employed to build the Pyramids.
Samiha's crew finally exposed the greatest area of the small city. They found shops, remnants of gathering places not unlike bars or coffee pubs of today. They found bakeries and even bell shaped pots in which breads were made.

They discovered a large auditorium like meeting room that when filled, comfortably entertained well over three hundred people. Even some of the chairs and benches were still intact.

Several months after the initial discovery Samiha strolled with Joseph through the narrow passageways of their find. They walked aimlessly through the labyrinth of rooms and easements, now illuminated by the light of the sun that shone through area where roofs had once covered almost everything.

They paused to admire art works of wall murals and stone carvings, and often stopped to dwell over the crafts of a society that clearly loved their art.

"This place has the scent of a very old culture," Joseph commented.
"Much, much older than anything I've ever seen." He added.
Samiha nodded in agreement. "Yes. In my own experience I have never witnessed a dig that seems to be so much older than anything like it in the entire area. It's strange, and even out of character. And these certainly do not have the appearance of slave quarters. Much the contrary. It appears that every effort had been made to create an atmosphere of comfort."

Suddenly a loud noise accompanied by urgent shouts stopped them in their tracks. They turned about to see one of the younger workers, a boy in his teens, as he ran full speed to catch up to them, shouting Samiha's name as he desperately begged for her attention. The young digger was breathless when he finally reached them and fell to his knees. In his arms he clutched a device that had the strange appearance of something oddly familiar. Samiha knelt down to his aid and stroked his hair and brow.

"What is it my friend? What's so important that you have to run yourself sick?"
Joseph looked curiously at the device cradled in the young mans arms. It looked like a video camera, but strangely designed with a double sight to accommodate both eyes and much longer than any cam he'd ever seen.
"What's that?" Samiha asked him.

The boy was clearly exhausted from his running. He breathed deeply several times before replying.
"I found this... buried under a rotten door track, back there, in one of the larger rooms."
"*Under* the door track?" she echoed.
"Yes. Neatly buried over a half arm's length deep."

Samiha could not conceal her astonishment as she wondered about his discovery. Here was a piece of sophisticated equipment, obviously the product of advanced technological design, found buried beneath a old doorway track that took thousands of years to rot away.

She rose to her feet and helped the young man up.

"Come. Show me where you found this."

Chapter Two

Joseph and Samiha worked well into the night together, cleaning the years of crusty sand and dirt from the device.

"You know, don't you what we have here?" Joseph remarked. "This machine or whatever it is couldn't have been made by local residents. Technology of this sort didn't exist that long ago."

She didn't look at him, but continued to pick away at small particles of granulated rock and petrified wood, that had long ago, adhered to the transparent lenses on either end of the baffling machine. All the while her mind raced with a struggle to make some kind of sense of it. Already their efforts had managed to clean almost all of it, until it now looked as new as it did when first manufactured. In fact, it looked too good. Not a single scratch could be found on its entire eighteen inches of length. It had no defined seams, no switches or buttons of any kind, and it had the feel of a metallic plastic unlike anything either of them had ever touched before.

There was a large four inch lens at the opposite end of a form and on the other end a double eye extrusion with a subtle slope in the center for the nose bridge rest.
Finally, she looked up at her friend and nodded her head in agreement.

"Yes, it's very old. But do you know what you're suggesting? First of all we have to assume that from what we're already positive about, that hole in the ground we just uncovered hasn't been disturbed in at least five thousand years, and most likely much longer.

"And, for a little icing on the cake, this thing was found in a place that could only have been buried purposely, *before* the doorway was even constructed. Perhaps *while* it was being built. So, what we have here looks like a very cumbersome binocular of some sort, only those kind of things weren't invented until a long time later."

Her friend grinned widely at her.

"Fantastic, isn't it?" He bubbled like a kid looking at a Christmas tree.

"Very," she replied.
"But what does it do? And why? And who put it there?" She stopped wiping its smooth surface for a moment as her thoughts drifted.

"We must get Luke," she announced.

At Loyola University in Chicago , on the other side of the world, Luke Ozman was conducting a lecture on Egyptology.

"Radio carbon dating suggests that some of the pyramids were built much sooner that what is generally believed. Some date back or an origin over twenty-five thousands years. Other evidence points to the possibility that they were not just constructed to serve as tombs or monuments to the Kings that are attributed to building them, and that perhaps they were used with other purposes in mind."

The lecturer was a tall, slender, good looking middle aged man whose slightly thinning hair showed traces of graying around the sides above his ears. Lines in his forehead and around his eyes accented an expression that reflected many years of research, study and wisdom.
One of his students interrupted him when she raised her arm and waved to get his attention.

"Yes Susan?"
"Sir," she began,
 "I beg to differ with you, but I was always taught from religion classes that the pyramids were built only five thousand years ago."
Luke Ozman nodded respectfully.

"And what exactly, did your religion classes teach you about them?"
"That they were built by slaves under the direction of the pharaohs of the time."

Luke nodded patiently.

"And what religion are you Susan, if you don't mind me asking."

"I'm Catholic, sir."

Her instructor walked through the aisles of desks and students as he continued to speak. He started to pick his next words very carefully.

"I sincerely believe that one of the prerequisites to objective learning should be *unlearning*. A little like re-tilling the grounds of our minds, and removing all of the weeds. As it is, the mind is very fertile soil for lots of weeds, in fact it could be described as pastures of them as far as the eye can see.

"Your religious teachers probably taught you many things. And I'd venture to assume that most of these things were also taught to them, by their own teachers. But as a scientist and archeologist, I have to remind you that the very existence of dinosaur bones totally contradicts many of the beliefs and accepted truths of the actual dates and age of the Earth. Things we've discovered over the years, substantiated time lines and age testing prove beyond a shadow of doubt that the Earth has been here much longer than organized religions would have us believe.

"Discoveries of human remains and dwellings that were constructed many thousands of years ago, some of very sophisticated design, tell us a different version of the history of mankind as we know it.

"Some religions teach us that the world is only five thousand years old, yet far too much evidence tells scientists that such an assumption is totally contrary to all existing proof.

"The point I'm getting at, is that all of us, barring very few, have accepted what we believe to be true based entirely on second-hand knowledge... learned knowledge, passed down from one generation to another, most of it on remnants of the real facts, by-products of information most likely tainted and distorted with subjective assumption. Few of us in our entire lives, ever investigate what we're taught. Only scientists do that and even they are severely limited by several important factors. They only believe what they can see, for one, and, they base their assumptions and findings completely upon their current tools of measurement and perceptive evaluation."

"But what else is there?" asked a young man seated near the front of the room.
 "How else can anyone judge what a given thing is without some concrete physical evidence or tool for comparison, and like you said, measurement?"

"Very good question," Luke offered.
 "When the microscope was invented we started to believe in things we couldn't see before. Until then, it was considered highly unscientific to believe in anything one could not see. And current tools of measurement, as Einstein pointed out to us, are far too subjective to be accurate. Very profound authors of our time, Echart Toole and Joel Goldsmith describe everything we discern as filtered through five very limited senses. Those senses, sight, smell, taste, touch and hearing are all faculties of body. *The*

mind on the other hand, has displayed characteristics and facilities that far exceed the boundaries of physicality.

"Now let me ask you a question. Do you believe in God?"

The young man nodded. "Yes I do."
"Why?" Luke asked him.
The young man hesitated for a moment then smiled
. "I guess because I was taught to."
Luke smiled. "Exactly my point!
"Now I'm not here to dilute anyone's religious ideologies, so let's not dwell too much on that subject. A good staunch religious background with beliefs is important in our society and very well needed and respected.
"What I will say, however, is that *beliefs create behavior*, and behavior usually creates differences that lead to conflict, borders, laws, traditions, and most of all, wars. Religious inquisitions locked up Galileo for professing that the Earth was not flat, killed countless numbers of people over the centuries in its name and distorted historical fact to preserve traditional beliefs.
 "This planet has been here some four thousand million years, yet what's the date on our calendars?"

The class was suddenly interrupted by an urgent knock on the door. An older lady, one of the office staff entered the room and approached the instructor with a note.

Chapter Three

"Sorry Luke," she said as she handed him the note.
"There's a long distance call for you in the main office." Her
arched eyebrows told him that it was very important.

"You are all dismissed," he announced to the class, then hurriedly
followed her out.
After he took the call Luke stood before the Dean in his office,
while the other, a much older gentleman peered at Luke over the
top of very old horned rim glasses. The look on the Dean's face
was anything but tolerant but he listened as Luke explained.

"Samiha was very persistent and she's not the kind of person
who'd make a request without a very solid reason. In fact I've
never heard her speak with so much urgency. She swore to me
that she's convinced that her crew uncovered something that will
raise a lot of interest throughout the archeological society, and I
believe her.

"If what she's found is that important it would work wonders for
the university's image. We could finally get the kind of respectful
recognition we deserve and maybe even more sponsors."

The Dean pursed his lips and stared at Luke with suspicious eyes.
He'd heard this kind of sales pitch several times before but rarely
had them result in anything more than mediocre discoveries.

"I'm well aware of how you and your team have influenced the
image of the university. I'm more concerned with how much
more this is going to cost us. Promises like these aren't new to
me, and while I'll grant that you and your people have made
some contributions that have managed to keep the budget dogs at
bay, let me remind you of the many fiascos...."

Luke raised his right hand up to interrupt him.

"Sir, this time I have a very strong feeling that we're *really* onto something. Samiha was as sincere as any person could be and I'm absolutely certain that she believes that they've stumbled upon a unique find. She wasn't at liberty to elaborate over the phone, but I know her very well and I'll stake anything on the fact that what she's found will more than make up for all of our past not-so-great discoveries.

"Trust me on this one. I need to get over there!"
The Dean's expression never changed.

"I won't authorize the funding for your trip to see her, so you can stop begging right now. That's not going to happen. But I won't get in your way either. If you want to take a leave of absence for a couple of weeks and go on your own, you have my blessing. Go ahead. But this kind of short notice for what can very well turn out to be one more of your lost causes is far too vague to take to the budget committee.

"But if you decide to go, on your own, on your own time, using your own money, go right ahead. But I still want to be kept abreast of what's going on. Now get out of here."

Luke started to say something else but the Dean raised his both of his own hands up.

"Enough. If you're so sure about this and you come back with something useful I'll see to it that you're compensated and reimbursed. Now leave. I have other things to do."

Chapter Four

Samiha greeted her friend with a long, warm hug.

"Thanks for coming, Luke. How was your flight?"
"Unbearable! I absolutely despise airplanes and especially dislike lengthy airplane rides. Thank God for booze."

Samiha smiled at him and kissed him on the cheek.
"I told you about my project manager, and engineer, Joseph?" she asked as she waved an introductory hand in her companion's direction.

Joseph pumped his hand vigorously with both of his own, and grinned from ear to ear.
"She mentions your name with every breath!" he proclaimed as he reached for Luke's carry on bag.
Luke smiled at him. It was an immediate friendship.

"The Dean gave me his usual productivity lecture and reminded me of how some of our past enterprises didn't turn out as well as we expected," Luke told her as they walked to the terminal exit.

"So this visit is unofficial. I'm on my own. I'd really like to bring back something that pleases that guy for a change. I wonder what he looks like with a smile on his face.
"Now show me what you had me come all this way to see," Luke said.

Luke could hardly contain his astonishment when Samiha handed him the strange cam devise. She relayed to him how and where it had been discovered.
He held the machine in his hands gingerly, studying it, while inwardly marveling at the thoughts of its possible origin and builders.

"Very impressive!" he said.

"You know, many years ago as a kid, my dad used to subscribe to the magazine Popular Science, which I always looked forward to reading every month. I remember one article, that stuck with me all these years, and now after seeing this, my first thought is about that article, which described a very unique find.

"Divers brought up artifacts from a sunken ship that was determined to have gone down some two thousands years earlier in Mediterranean Sea, off the coast of Alexandria . One of the objects they retrieved was something that looked like this, according to the description I recall.

"All attempts to figure it out, the article explained, proved fruitless. It was very smooth to the touch like this one, and made from indefinable materials, again, like this one, and when attempts were made to cut it open, drill it, pry it and pound on it, nothing worked.

"Eventually they tried x-raying it and that proved most baffling of all. Because what they were able to see were a series of sophisticated gears and a symmetrically designed configuration of what appeared to be a map of our solar system."

"What became of it?" Samiha asked him.
"It was reportedly lost in a fire," he answered.
"Unfortunately, it couldn't withstand a lot of heat."

Samiha ushered her two friends out onto the balcony of her home, where she served them a tray of hummus, Arabian idemmus and falafel bread. She set the food on a patio table between Joseph and Luke, and urged Luke to continue.

"Go on. What did they ever deduce from this discovery?"

Luke shook his head.
"I don't know. I never read or heard another thing about it."
Luke continued to turn the machine over and over in his hands.

He studied the lens at the rear of the machine and the larger one
at the other end and noted that they were of a thickness
uncommon to any he'd ever seen. He was completely at a loss for
any explanation for why there were no buttons, or switches that
would provide control.

Like one would do with a pair of binoculars, he raised the object
to his eyes and looked through it, hoping for a hint to its function.

"It doesn't magnify." he reported,
 "And it doesn't appear to do much more than a simple window
would do."

Joseph leaned toward him and looked closer at the machine.

"Whatever it is," he began in heavily accented English,
"the fact remains that this is a very significant find. Our
disturbance of the depths of the grounds where it was discovered,
proves beyond any doubt, that those areas had gone untouched
for many thousands of years."

Luke lowered the cam down to his lap and looked at Joseph,
while thinking of how to reply.

"I figured that part out already, my new friend. Relax. I don't
believe that this thing was bought at some electronics store and
planted there, and I wouldn't be here now talking to you if I
thought for an instant that Samiha's call to me was anything less
than very important."

Then he smiled at him and hefted the cam back up to his line of
vision while shifting his right hand to support the machine from
underneath. As soon as his fingers touched the underside of the
device, quite suddenly, he began to feel a strange vibration.

The cam began to pulsate, at first ever so slightly, then gradually
increasing in intensity until it started to emit a low pitched
humming sound.

"What is that?" Samiha shouted.
Joseph stood up abruptly, shocked by the noise and knocked over
the chair he'd been sitting in.
Luke had extended his hold on the machine at arms length, also
very surprised but held it without wavering his firm grip. Then he
moved it closer and once again looked through the double eye
protrusions.
His expression was one of dumfounded shock.

"Holly lord!" he exclaimed.
"I'm seeing something!"
"What is it?" Samiha screamed as she watched her friend react
strangely as he peered into the devise.

Luke ignored her for the moment, then looked up from the
machine, toward the distant terrain out over the balcony. His
mouth dropped open in disbelief and for the next few moments
he looked back into the machine, then again out onto the horizon
and back to the machine again several times, in quick succession.

"You're not gonna believe this!" he muttered excitedly.
 "The images I'm seeing are right out there, in the distance, but
the landscape, although generally the same, is slightly different.
The buildings are gone, but the mountain ranges are still there,
and I can see movement through the cam that's not going on
here!"

He handed the device to Samiha.
 "Take a look for yourself."
She accepted the machine and as soon as it was comfortably in
her hands the humming subsided and the vibration stopped.
"What happened?" she asked.
 "It's turned itself off!"

Luke shook his head in confusion and took the machine back.
"You must have touched something that shut it down," he
surmised as he turned the machine over and looked at the

underside. Then he raised it back up to his sights and touched the base, and once again it came to life.

"That's it," he announced.
"It seems to respond when you touch the bottom of it."

The base of the machine was about a foot in length and about five inches wide and was a perfect rectangle of smooth flat surface. "This must be where the controls are. We can't see them, but since it reacts when I touch any area within it, that has to be the way it operates."

Luke raised it to his line of vision again and this time experimented by touching different spots within the rectangle while looking out over the balcony.
"This is absolutely unbelievable!" he exclaimed.

"For every different place I touch under here, a different image appears through the viewfinder. The landscape is always the same, except for minor variations, but everything else changes." Joseph and Samiha just looked at him in awe.

"How could this be?" Samiha ventured.
"That something buried for so long could come back to life, in working order yet...."
Luke interrupted her with a wave of his hand.

"Tomorrow morning, at first light, we'll visit your dig. Show me around the area and especially the location where this was found."

Two men strolled nonchalantly near the outer rim of the quarantined area surrounding the dig site. Their long white robes and golden skin were typical of the inhabitants of the region. One man was distinguishably older than the other and did most of the talking as they walked.

"And so as we knew one day it would happen, the machine was discovered." He said.

"And now it will be interesting to watch as the next events unfold." He paused for a moment as if searching his mind for a long past recollection. Then he went on.

"This same kind of discovery occurred to our homeland ancients just before the great celestial collision that forced our people to scatter for their lives. Finding it was a blessing, and then a curse, and then when its perceived value was eventually outgrown for greater truth, it was hidden just as was done here.

"So we'll watch without intercession and see where this new knowledge leads our brothers."

The younger man posed a question.

"Will their coming experiences take them to the level of understanding with us?"

The older one just stared at the path before him for a long moment before replying.

"All things are gently planned for the greater good. But before I answer your question of whether it will take them to our level of understanding it's important to point out that except for a small number of them, they have no recollection of *The Source.* Even if brief glimpses of the experience of *Source* have occurred, their conception of it becomes filtered and distorted by their own subjective beliefs.

"Some have terms they use to define *Source,* like Mother Nature or God.

"Their beliefs and their deeply rooted convictions about everything are entirely based upon what they think they perceive. This limited and misconstrued perception is only now beginning to dawn upon them within certain circles of their study.

"Some of them have experienced the Presence of *Source* and as such, their lives were instantly turned about from the typical attractions of want and need to a deeper connection with *Source*. They even admit to the possibility of their limited perception and all they believe is little more than a passing dream."

"And what will finally awaken them?" The younger aged.

The older one smiled.

"The same thing that awakens any of us. The evolutionary process of experience and the application of learning to practice and apply what they refer to as forgiveness."

❧

Chapter Five

Scores of laborers were already busy at the site by the time the
three arrived the next morning. Samiha led the way down an
ancient stone staircase and into a series of connected rooms, now
sheltered only by the sky above.

"We ascertained," she began,
 "that this particular section of rooms was built as an outdoor area
to the much larger quarters just adjacent to it. We believe that
here was the place where foods were prepared for both, the
residents of the *Housing for the Gods*, as it was called, and the
workers who built the surrounding pyramids and dwelling
structures.

She pointed to a large room, lined on one wall with low benches
made from stone and separated by narrow troughs.

"This is where they cleaned their fish," she continued,
 "and sometimes cattle. We found small fragmental remains of
animal bones imbedded into the Tafla clay."

Luke nodded in acknowledgement, marveling at the size and
relatively well-preserved condition of the site. He and Joseph
follow her in silence as she led them deeper through the long
passageway and to the area where the cam had been found.

After a few minutes she stopped at the entrance of another very
large room. The entrance had once supported a door of
remarkable size and width. Judging from the distance between
the walls and the remnants of the track beneath it, all indications
pointed to the fact that it had been built into the wall, rather than
to swing on hinges. The timbers originally used to construct it
were now long gone, rotted away by thousands of years of decay.
Samiha pointed to a spot where diggers had left a deep cavity in
the floor of the door jam.

"It was found right there," she told Luke.
He dropped down to one knee and looked into the hole as he searched the interior with his hands.

"Someone purposely hid it here!" he announced,
"because the door would have completely concealed it."
Joseph nodded in agreement.
"That's exactly what we thought."
Luke looked up at Samiha and asked,
"Have you allowed any further digging in this spot?"
"Absolutely not," she quickly replied.
"I thought it best to wait for you."

Luke continued to stretch his arms deeper into the crevice, loosening the soil and straining it with his fingers. He removed small portions of the dirt, one handful at a time, inspecting it, then returning for more. After a few minutes he discovered a small object. It looked like a very thick needle, some four inches in length with its tip ending in what looked like a tiny arrowhead, and the opposite end built in a ring loop, large enough to accommodate a finger.

He handed it to Samiha who studied it curiously.
"What do you suppose that is?" he asked her.
Samiha shook her head and passed the object to Joseph.

"It appears to be made of the same material as the machine," he observed.
"It's the same color and has the same feel to it."

Luke continued to furrow out small quantities of dirt and sand for another few minutes, then decided to stop.

"Samiha, I want you to put a trusted digger on this area. Have him search it well, from one end to the other, and immediately bring us whatever he finds. For now, let's go back to your place and see if we can make some sense out of that thing."

Joseph chipped carefully at the sand and aged material that adhered to the surface of the needle like object, while Samiha and Luke talked together on the balcony.

"You mentioned the article on the machine they found in that ship wreck. Well, after you told us about it, I recalled a similar event that was recorded by one of the principal discoverers of the Sodmein Cave ."

"The Sodmein Cave ?" he asked.
"Yes," she replied.
"Where they found remains of a civilization proven to be over fifteen thousands years old."

"I remember reading about that find," Luke stated.
"They found tools, and camp sites and some interesting proof of intelligence that was never before believed to have existed. Strange carvings on the cave walls that depicted aircraft."

"Yes," Samiha agreed, and she went on,
"The cave was just south of the river Thebes , near a town called Qoseir, and many of the things they found raised some very controversial questions.

"One of the workers on the original dig was my cousin, who relayed to her family the story of a strange object that was found tucked in a hidden crevice of one of the walls. Now that I think back, her description of that object finally makes sense to me. She was trying to describe something that looked just like our machine here."

"Are you sure?" Luke asked her.
She nodded.
"I could never associate her account with anything logical until now, and yes, I'm sure of it. This is how she described it."

"What became of the machine they found?" Luke asked.

Samiha shrugged her shoulders.

"As far as I can remember, the authorities acquired it and no mention was ever made of it again. I never really gave it another thought until now."

Luke was obviously perplexed.

"So let's review what we've learned so far," he began.

"Number one, a working machine that does something, but we haven't figured out just what yet. We know that it has come kind of special capability because of the differences in what we're able to see when we look through it.

"To make matters a little more confusing, we each have accounts of similar machines found in the past, and both in locations that suggest that they were possessed by ancients, and both discovered in equally strange locations.

"I suppose we can consider ourselves lucky."

Samiha stared at him curiously.

"Lucky, why?"

"Because, although we don't yet know what the machine does, at least it works! All we need to do now is find out how and for what purpose."

ॐ

Chapter Six

Luke tinkered with the machine all morning and well into the
early afternoon. He and his friends strolled through the hills
nearby stopping occasionally to sit and peer through the
viewfinder at different areas of the surrounding landscape.

From time to time they'd pass the machine to one another, taking
turns looking through it as Luke struggled with thoughts on the
possibilities for how it was designed to work, and for what
reasons.

Then an idea occurred to Luke, and he stopped suddenly, as if
frozen in the moment.

"What is it Luke?" Joseph asked him.
He began to smile, first slightly, then with more enthusiasm as he
snapped his fingers.

"I got it!" he announced.
"I know what it does now!"
"Well, share it with us," Samiha told him.
"Do you know what we're seeing every time we look into that
thing?" Samiha shrugged her shoulders.
"I dare not suggest. But go on. What are we seeing?"

New revelations seemed to flood Luke's mind with every passing
second and now he was beaming with delight.
"If I'm correct, this is incredible! What we're looking at every
time the landscape appears to change, is the past! We're looking
at the past! We're witnessing what the terrain was like long ago
during some other time!"

His friends stared at him with astonishment in their eyes.
Luke went on.

"Somehow, someway, someone built this thing with a capability of looking into the past and see what went on, right here, or any direction we point it to."

"How is that possible?" Samiha retorted.

"I think the hot sun is going to your head."

He smiled at her.

"No, I'm right about his. Bear with me a minute. Now think about this. We know that the Universe has been here some eleven billion years, and that the Earth itself, still relatively young, by comparison, was formed somewhere around four and a half billion years ago."

"Yes, so?"

"So," Luke continued,

"Our work, this archeology, the digging, the searching, everything we do along these lines, investigates events that arose and occurred on Earth long ago. Our tools and means of measurement of timely artifacts and discoveries have been very limited to the rare finds left behind, spared only by chance, from a long history of consistent disasters.

"This entire area here in the desert, was once teaming with lakes and rivers. The weather even experienced cold and ice. Many countless changes went on over the course of thousands of years, and I'm thinking right now as I look at this fantastic machine, that other archeologists, alien visitors from other worlds, also brought their own tools with them, and we're now in the possession of one of them.

"Here we are, living on one single tiny fragment of the Universe we call Earth, that spins around one star in a galaxy of billions, one galaxy among billions of others, all of which has been around eleven thousand million years, and what do we know of it? What do we know of true, Universal history?

"We live with horse blinders wrapped around our heads and spend more energy fighting one another over crumbs, when if we only opened our eyes the reality of how vast our real universe is, in its entirety, we'd look at ourselves as children playing in a sandbox.

"I'm guessing that a human like intelligence permeates the entire universe, and that we're all part of a great big family. I'm thinking that many of our cousins and other family members, have long since exceeded any known degree of mankind's evolution as we know it, and have achieved technological advancements that have enabled some of them move around in areas of their accessible domain where we haven't yet.

"Just look at what we've accomplished in only the past hundred years or so. We've come from covered wagons to space travel and DNA in just that short span of time. One hundred measly years! The time it takes to blink your eyelashes in comparison to the millions and millions of years of true Universal time."

Luke paused for a moment, as his friends remained silent. He stroked the machine in his lap as if it were a pet.

"This machine can see into the past. It can do so, because it was built to transfer images from something much bigger, like a super Hubble perhaps. Maybe even a vast multitude of Super Hubbles that exist out there in space at great distances."

"What are you saying?" Samiha asked him.

Luke continued.
"Think about it for a minute. Every time you look up at the night sky and the stars, what do you see? When you gaze at the glimmering specs of light up there, what are you actually looking at?"

"I don't follow you, Luke," she replied.

"You're looking at the past!" He emphasized.
"You're looking at light that aside from our own star, the Sun, took at the bare minimum, two and half years to reach us. And

that's just from the closest star to us. Some stars are so distant, that millions of years ago they might have gone out and died. Yet we still see their light. Some of the sky we see right now, may not even be there! But the fact remains, that whatever celestial glimmer of star twinkling we look at from here, what we are witnessing occurred in the past."

"Interesting logic." Joseph offered.
"And quite correct. So what you're suggesting is that an alien civilization, the ones who built this machine, left it here, possibly during one of their own archeological expeditions?"

"Does anything else make more sense?" Luke asked him.
"Look at what our own Hubble is able to do. We've made advancements in high-resolution camera technology, that mounted on from space, can actually read newspaper print and count the hairs on your head if need be. The eyes in the sky have most of us on camera an average of three times every single day! So if a higher advanced technology developed even more powerful Hubbles, and looked down on us here on Earth, from their vast distances, the things they saw would appear to be happening right now."

Samiha looked at him with new attention.
"And this machine," she began, "would serve as a receiver that transferred those images to it, from out there!"

"Exactly!" Luke proclaimed.
"What they'd be looking at would be events that happened long ago, perhaps thousands and even millions of years ago.

"Yes, but Luke, what you're suggesting would require an infinite number of these so-called 'Super Hubbles'. They'd have to be positioned all over the place. Millions and millions of them!" Luke looked at her with smiling eyes.

"If you're suggesting that such a thing is impossible, then I'll have to disagree with you. Disagree very emphatically. What do *we* know of infinity? All we have are the tools of measurement that we ourselves created in our own three dimensional workshops. I'm positive that a more seasoned and polished intelligence, one experienced in this particular line of technology may well be very capable of surpassing our own, and building tools better than the ones we've created so far.

"I labeled them 'Super-Hubbles' and immediately we associate that description with a series of very large cumbersome telescopes that float in space. But what if our creators of these machines didn't need to build them quite so large in order to accomplish even greater tasks? What if their level of technology is so great, so far beyond our own, that a Super Hubble of their making might fit on the head of a pin?

"Remember when computers were the size of office buildings or the cell phone was something large and so heavy it had to be carried around with a shoulder strap?
"What if their Hubbles are the size of micro-chips? Think about it. If they are, then how much less difficult would it be to scatter them, as you said, all over the place?

"Don't forget, we know absolutely zero about their means of navigation...of how they were able to move about through space. But if we were to make a calculated speculation based solely upon the many eye witness accounts of UFO's that dart across the sky at breakneck speeds, what do you suppose they could accomplish in space, uninhibited by an atmosphere?
"This is a very sophisticated portable receiver.

"With portable receivers like this one, their landing parties would be equipped with everything they needed to study climatic patterns of activity, previous weather conditions, and whatever else they used it for."

"But then what this also means," Samiha offered, "is that if we knew how to operate this thing correctly, we could view everything that ever happened here on Earth, for as far back as when these Super Hubbles went into use."

"That's right," Luke agreed.

"We could point it in any given direction, and as you said, if we knew how to calibrate it's settings, we could tune it in to any prescribed time and see, as if we were there now, anything that went on, just the reverse effect of when we look up at the stars. This thing receives the images transferred from something much more powerful out there!"

ॐ

Chapter Seven

As the sun began to set over the quarantined site the older wise man continued to elaborate. His younger comrade listened inventively.

"Our brethren here on Earth spend every waking moment of their days reacting. For most of them, unaware of the connectedness of all and everything, their individually perceived lives are literally wasted in a continuous pattern of every sort of reacting. They experience what they define as 'feeling bad,' or guilty, mad, defeated, bored, scared, inferior, embarrassed, annoyed, lonely or superior and condescending.

"And within those activities they inadvertently feed and strengthen their illusory world, maintaining it, justifying it and keeping them deeper and deeper in sleep.
"Unaware of the *Source of All Power* they created an opposite force. Fear. And from this fear are endless beliefs in the need to defend or attack."

The younger man nodded his head in agreement.
"Yes. We witness this in all of their behavior." He commented, then continued,

"But I take it that it is your conviction that our Earthly brothers will eventually transcend these wasteful and distractive habits of theirs. That the means to do so, this application of forgiveness as you described it can lead them to evolve to the level of consciousness necessary to realize who they really are."

"Yes." The elder agreed, and he went on;
"I am convinced of this. Only because it must happen to them as it's occurred to all of us. And while several of their kind have been successful with efforts to share this truth over the past several thousand of their perceived years, there is still much for them to unlearn."

❧

Joseph had finished cleaning the needle like object Luke found earlier.

"It looks like something a person would use to spear an olive," he said to Luke as he handed to him. Luke smiled at the thought and passed it to Samiha. She took it out on the balcony and set it down on the table where the cam devise rested, and visually compared it. The odd gray colored metal/plastic casing was obviously made of the same material used in the manufacture of the needle. The finger loop at the end suggested a way to hold the needle without dropping it while in use.

Luke joined her on the balcony and took a seat next to her. He picked up the needle with one hand and cam devise in his other, then turned the machine over until the underside pointed upward. On a hunch, he touched the base of the machine with the tip of the needle and instantly it began to vibrate.

"It's worked with the needle!" he remarked excitedly. Then he raised the machine up to his line of vision and gently began to run the end of the needle along its base. After a moment, he displayed a grin from ear to ear.

"So that's how it's supposed to work!" Luke lowered the machine and looked at Samiha.
"Confucius say, don't use an axe to kill a fly."
"What?" Samiha asked quizzically.

He smiled at her.
"We've been touching the base of the machine with our fingers, and what's been happening is although a different image appears when I move my hand along the bottom, doing it like that isn't accurate and not the way it was designed to perform correctly. With the needle, everything is a lot more precise.

"I'm going to test it a little more, but from what I can tell so far, by moving the needle forward, I'm able to tune in to a more specific time. This may be the key to its operation."

"Let me have that thing," she demanded. Luke handed the cam devise to her, then the needle which she attached to her right fore finger. Then she carefully lifted the machine up to her line of sight and looked through it while gently touching the underside with the needle. In an instant her eyes bulged in astonishment.

"Oh my God!" she shouted.
"I'm looking at the three of us as we walked together earlier, out there in the hills!"

"Really?" Joseph exclaimed.
"Yes! Wow! This is amazing! As I move the needle toward me it's like I'm rewinding a tape!"

She stayed glued to the scene for some time before she finally lowered the machine to her lap and looked over at Luke.
"My friend," she began solemnly, "we have without a doubt, discovered the single greatest archeological find of all time!"
Luke nodded to her.
"Yeah, binoculars that can see through time. A time ocular. And probably the closest contemporary version of Pandora's Box."

The three of them sat around the table on the balcony and talked together well into the evening. Samiha and Joseph were still quite flabbergasted over the experiences of the day.

"Are the implications starting to sink in?" Luke asked them.
"You mean the vast possibilities with this Time Ocular, as you called it?" Samiha asked him.
"Yes, very much so.
"The very idea that I could actually witness events like the Crucifixion of Jesus, or the actual construction of the Pyramids... it boggles the mind."

"Yes. It does," Luke agreed, and he went on,

"I'm sure that if we all put our heads together and started to comprise a list of all of the entertaining possibilities, we would be here for a very long time. But there's a special implication that I am referring to, that doesn't include my immediate concern for a desire to find out what really happened to Baby Jane. Sure, that's one very worthwhile application, but there's one more that's even more important, and that is *the truth*, or the absence thereof.

"As you said, the possibilities are vast. Every bit of recorded history could now be either substantiated or proven a lie. No historical mistruth or fabrication could ever survive from this moment on.

"Are you starting to get my drift here?"

Joseph nodded and said,

"Put like that, this machine could very well open up more than just one can of worms. So what do we do with this great knowledge?"

"For now, we keep our mouths shut," Luke said.

"The fewer the number of people who know about this, the better. Just off the top of my head I can think of a lot of individuals who would kill their own mothers to know what we know now, and have what we have in that machine."

"Like who?" Samiha asked with a note of naivety that became her.

"Well, think about it. Just about anyone from seekers of lost gold mines to the very leaders of entire countries who may have done things they'd rather not have anyone know about."

Samiha sighed.

"I can think of many good, worthwhile uses for this Time Ocular. The benefits to the entire world could be endless."

"And I agree with you," Luke assured her.

"But if we're going to get the chance to use it for worthwhile purposes, we're gonna have to keep it to ourselves, at least for the present time."

The next morning, Luke was awakened by a sudden shaking. Samiha stood over him as he squirmed on the sofa, struggling to get the day into focus while she shouted his name and shook him again.
"Luke, wake up please!"

"What is it?" he asked as he gradually became accustomed to the morning sunlight.
"Look," Samiha exclaimed as she showed him a thin clay tablet about eight inches square, that had been broken with age, but still retained a clear image of an ancient carving.

Her shouting also awoke Joseph from the guest room, who stood in the doorway rubbing the sleep from his eyes.
Luke sat upright, took the tablet from her and started to examine the strange engraving.

"My man found this buried deeper in the crevasse, where the Ocular and the needle were found," Samiha explained.

Luke rose from the sofa and walked onto the balcony into the bright morning sunlight, and seated himself next to the patio table.

"Bring me some of your outstanding coffee please," he asked her as he began to look more closely at the markings on the tablet. Joseph joined him peering over Luke's shoulder at the newest find with great interest.

The image on the tablet was a meticulously carved series of seven circles that had been drawn in a row, from left to right. The first circle on the left was the largest, followed by the second which was the smallest. The third was created to appear slightly different from the others, with a trail of lines that connected it with the fifth circle and second largest. The third and fourth were of similar size but much smaller than the fifth, and the last one, slightly smaller than the largest explained the entire image. It had been carved with a distinct thin plane that went around the center of its circumference.

"Saturn," Luke muttered to himself.
Samiha returning shortly carrying a tray of cups, steaming coffee and a tray filled with homemade Arabian cookies.
Now fully awake, Luke studied the tablet with new interest. With his finger he traced the lines that connected the third circle with the fifth and largest as he thought about the meaning of the carving. This was obviously no idle depiction without purpose. "Whoever created this, was sending a significant message with a precise meaning."

His two friends sat in silence as they watched him concentrate in deep thought, as he examined the ancient rock. After years of working together with him, Samiha had long ago learned not to interrupt him during moments like these, but also taught her that what usually followed was logical and in depth evaluation that was rarely incorrect.

"This is the Sun," Luke announced, pointing at the largest circle on the left of the carving.
 "These are six of the planets, all drawn in proportion to their actual sizes, as best as they could be on this small slab of rock, but very explicitly defined. See how small Mercury is shown, and look here at the ring around Saturn."
They nodded in agreement as he continued.

"But these lines that appear to be coming away from Venus and leading to Jupiter, the largest of the planets, are strange. They seem to indicate a path or trail."

Luke paused and searched his recollection for a few moments then nodding his head slowly, with a look of conviction he glanced back up at his friends.

"Venus! The daughter of Jupiter," he announced.

"What did you say? What about Venus, Luke," Samiha whispered. Luke took a deep breath before continuing.

"If I'm right, and I have strong a feeling that I am, based on what I've studied on the matter, those lines *are* a trail, and a path of sorts. Bear with me for a minute.

"In several ancient texts, Venus is often referred to as the daughter of Jupiter and the origin of those depictions began, according to some very viable theories, with a comet that slammed into Jupiter millions of years ago, causing the now famous Big Red Spot on its surface.

"It's believed by some very noteworthy scientists and astronomers, that as a result of this tremendous calamity, a large chunk of Jupiter was ripped from its surface and sent reeling into space, toward the sun, and eventually settled into an orbit around it, between the Earth and Mercury.

"Right now as we speak, Venus is the only planet in our entire solar system that has all of the characteristics of a brand new member of our neighborhood. Its surface is completely and utterly volcanic and its atmosphere so thick with smoke and ash it makes it virtually impossible to see through. That's because compared to every other planetary body in our system, it has the appearance of being brand new, and still very much in the cooling off stages of early development.

"Now, when this comet crashed into Jupiter, creating this new body of matter, it had to pass the orbits of both Mars and the Earth. As the theory goes, Mars happened to be in the worst place at the worst time. When the newly born Venus passed it, a lot of the showering debris created in its wake struck Mars, so violently that it literally destroyed its surface. It hit Mars so hard that water was knocked off the planet, vegetation and many life forms were completely blasted away.

"But, Mars also happened to be in the best possible position for the Earth, because as it took these shotgun blasts in the face, it saved the Earth from a similar fate. Very little debris made it here."

"This actually happened?" Samiha asked him.

"There's more and more proof of it every day." Luke continued. "Not long ago, in the mid nineties, astronomers actually watched as a comet, named *Shoemaker Levy Nine*, broke up into twenty-one separate pieces as it passed the orbit of Jupiter and was pulled into its gravitational field. This comet split up and once again, as millions of years before, pummeled the surface of Jupiter while dozens of scientists down here watched. If only one of those twenty-one pieces hit the Earth, none of us would be here now to talk about it. So the assumption and the theory of the possibility of a comet slamming into Jupiter was no longer just speculation. They witnessed it this time, as it actually happened.

"The surface of Mars on one side is much more ridden with craters and signs of asteroid crashes than the other, which used to baffle scientists, until it was accepted that the side hit the most, occurred all at once with a sudden barrage, like a drive-by machine gun attack.

"These lines on this ancient carving appear to verify that event. They appear to stream away from Jupiter from a long tail of rock and debris created by the newborn Venus, and left a lot destruction in its wake."

He patted the Ocular as he grinned at his friends. "Now we can see it as it actually happened. Maybe we can sell tickets."

ॐ

Chapter Eight

The two white robed men continued to talk together as the sun set over a distant mountain range. The elder was speaking again.

"Their current problem, the one most predominate in their collective psychological makeup is the tenacious value they place on what they believe to be their bodies."
"Having forgotten *The Source* their limited perception is solidified in the belief that the body is a kind of fence they imagined they built to separate parts of their Higher Self from other parts. It is within this fence they think they live, and to "die" as they refer to it."

"Their Higher Self remains out of their awareness and completely forgotten so long as the distractive identification with the body and all of its tendencies keep them immersed in illusion."
"Yet it is through trust in the Higher Self that a mediation between illusion and truth occurs. Their dreaming can be dispelled before the light of knowledge when they can get out of their own way. Once it is accepted that their bodies are not the 'authors' of all that comes into their awareness and they begin to trust the guidance of Higher Self, *Source* can once again, come through."

His younger companion nodded understandingly before commenting.

"And so this application of forgiveness as you described, is the means for which they can see the folly of deeply rooted misperception."

His statement was more like a question, and his elder friend smiled in agreement.

"Exactly right.." And he continued.

"This term of theirs called forgiveness (while Earthy definitions are numerous) refers to surrendering the belief in separation and their perceived notions of 'individual authorship.'

"But this process requires a reasonable degree of persistence and dedication. For most of the few of our brethren who have achieved this level of consciousness it came about only after they had finally been able to exchange every negative impulse, in every degree, from full blown rage and acute vindictiveness to mild irritation, into unconditional compassion.

"Our Earthly brothers have a term they use to define what they perceive as infractions of one kind or another, perpetrations of some sort of violation. They call it "sin."

"Forgiveness recognizes what you thought your brother did to you has not occurred. It does not pardon sins and make them real. It sees there was no sin. And in this view are all your sins forgiven. What is sin except a false idea about *Source's* Son? Forgiveness merely sees its falsity, and therefore lets it go. What then is free to take its place is now the Will of The *Source*.

"An unforgiving thought is one which makes a judgment that it will not raise to doubt, although it is not true. The mind is closed, and will not be released. The thought protects projection, tightening its chains, so that distortions are more veiled and more obscure; less easily accessible to doubt, and further kept from reason. What can come between a fixed projection and the aim that it has chosen as its needed goal?

An unforgiving thought does many things. In frantic action it pursues its goal, twisting and overturning what it sees as interfering with its chosen path. Distortion is its purpose and the means by which it would accomplish it as well. It sets about its furious attempts to smash reality, without concern for anything that would appear to pose a contradiction to its point of view.

Forgiveness, on the other hand, is still, and quietly does nothing. It offends no aspect of reality, nor seeks to twist it to appearance that it likes. It merely looks and waits and judges not. He who would not forgive must judge, for he must justify his failure to forgive. But he who would forgive himself must learn to welcome truth, exactly as it is.

"Do nothing, then, and let forgiveness show you what to do through Higher Self Who is the Guide, your Savior and Defender, strong in hope, and certain of your ultimate success. He has forgiven you already, for such is His function, given Him by *Source*. Now must one share His function, and forgive whom He has saved, whose sinlessness He sees, and whom He honors as the Son of *Source*."

Jacob Haleem shivered violently while he attempted to keep warm as best he could, by holding his knees close to his chest. The jail cell was very cold and damp. Faint lighting from a tiny barred window high overhead was the only indication that separated the day from the darkness of night. He was very frightened.

Earlier that day, heavily armed government police raided his mother's home, and dragged him away. His poor mother's screams of protest went unheard as they beat him unmercifully, and drove away with him.

Now, dried blood matted the hair on his head, and his mouth and eyes were swollen and blackened with bruises. Tears streamed uncontrollably down his cheeks as he struggled to understand why this was happening to him.

Soon loud noises of approaching guards filled the halls outside his cell. The clanging of large keys and the loud boisterous shouts sent him scurrying into a corner. Petrified with fear, his body trembled and his breath came and went in short bursts. Then the door of his cell slammed open and he cried out in terror when six guards lifted him to his feet, beating him as they laughed and cursed.

"You're gonna tell us all about the thing you found," the captain of the force demanded as he slammed a fist into the boys face. The boy crumbled at their feet and was immediately yanked back up and the demand repeated.

"What did you find buried in that ditch? We heard about it. You're not leaving here until you tell us everything!"

Two more quick blows to his neck and head followed by other guards and the young boy reeled back, striking his head violently on the stone wall behind him. He slumped into a lifeless heap at their feet, silent now, his breath completely cut off.

The Captain looked down at him and grabbed a handful of his hair and turned his face over to look into his eyes.

"Shit! He's dead."
"Dead?" One of the other guards echoed with a look of discouragement.
"Damn!" The captain muttered. "We're in trouble now."

❧

Chapter Nine

I don't believe this!" shouted a civilian authority at the police chief. "I ask you to question the kid, and your idiot guards kill him?"

The chief shook his head apologetically.
 "They told me he was very uncooperative and that he fought with them. What were they supposed to do?"

The civilian paced the floor with his hands folded behind his back. He stopped abruptly directly in front of the chief and pressed his face very close to the others. He was enraged.

"What you were supposed to do is exactly what I said! Just what I tell you, nothing more. If I tell you to jump face first off a ten-story building that's what you do. Your sole existence depends on your not eating, sleeping, or breathing until whatever I tell you to do gets done. Are we quite clear on this?"

The Chief of Police trembled and backed away from him.

"I'm dreadfully sorry about this. I was told it was an accident, nothing more."
The civilian just glared at him while he contemplated his next words.
 "The child told them nothing?"
"Nothing sir."

The civilian turned away from him in disgust. He contemplated his next words carefully before continuing.

"When the boy's family comes to claim the body you will tell them that he was involved in a fight with other inmates and was killed. Make sure that your idiots collaborate the story, because if I get so much as a whisper of inconsistency or, if from this

moment on, things don't go exactly as I like, you and your entire crew will be shoveling shit by tomorrow morning.
"Now get out of my sight!"

Samiha wept uncontrollably as Joseph tried desperately to console her. When Luke returned from a day of research at the site of the dig he was surprised to find them both in tears.
"What happened?" he demanded.

"They killed that poor boy!" Samiha cried.
Luke glanced anxiously at Joseph.
"What boy? Why?"
"The young man who found the Time Ocular," Joseph replied sadly, and he went on,
"He must have mentioned about it to some of his friends. Word of what he'd found got back to the authorities, and questions were asked. Many workers were interrogated and finally they centered their investigation on the boy, who they took in for further questioning."

"But he knew nothing!" sobbed Samiha, as she continued to wail in grief.
"What authorities?" Luke asked him.
"Who was asking the questions?"
"I'm not exactly sure what agency it is," Joseph explained.
"But it's a contingency of more than one, made up of representatives from several different areas, and for a long time now, our efforts have been under strict scrutiny from these people.

"They demand to be informed of every discovery, no matter what. We're ordered to report every new find as soon as it happens."

Luke approached Samiha and knelt down beside her. He stroked her long black hair and held her close to his chest. He was silent in thought for a long time, then finally he rose to his feet and spoke softly.

"This is what I meant when I said that there are those who would stop at nothing to find out what we'd discovered, and get their hands on it."

He spoke through angered clenched teeth as he continued. "You stay here. Watch over Samiha and don't answer the door for anyone but me. It's just a matter of time before they get around to questioning you. I'll be back as soon as I can."

Luke packed the Ocular into an overnight shoulder bag and concealed the needle in his wallet.
In the village, he was able to hail a taxi to the busiest market place, not unlike a shopping mall found in the United States , but very much outdoors and what locals would define as *the tunnel*, the closest English interpretation.

It was a long narrow stretch of merchant displays that highlighted everything from food and drink to clothing, jewelry and appliances of every sort. Refreshment stands of a wide variety offered everything from Turkish coffee to beer and snacks. Luke stopped at a shop that sold high tech camera and video equipment. He strolled through the aisles of products before being approached by a sales girl.

"May I help you find something sir?" she asked him.
Luke smiled at her and nodded.
"Yes you can." And he went on,
"I have a particular request that may sound a little strange to you. Do you mind?"
"Not at all, sir. Please, if I can help in any way I will certainly try."

Luke continued. "I have a unique camcorder here that is what you might refer to as an experimental model. I'm sure you're not familiar with it."
"Really?" Who's the manufacturer?" she asked.
"Some older builders that are a lot smarter than I," Luke commented with a grin.

"Well, what I want to do is find another video recorder whose lens can fit over this one, and I'll connect the two to work as one."
He showed her the Time Ocular then, removing it from his bag.

"Wow!" she exclaimed.
"That is different. Two extrusions! It looks like a very odd set of binoculars. May I ask you a question?"
"Of course."
"Why would you want to attach the two of them together?"
"I knew you'd ask that," Luke replied.
"It kind of like an experiment I'm attempting. Far too complicated to explain. Do you think you might have something that would fit?"

She pondered his question for a moment, then nodded.
"I think I have just the thing. This way."

She led him down to the very end of an aisle and the lower shelf of a little used display. She knelt down and drew out a box that had the look of having been opened several times before.

"Sir, this is an older version, one of the very first made, and by now, I have to admit, virtually sale-proof because of its obsolete functioning. If it'll work for you I'll give you a good deal on it."

Luke smiled at her honesty and listened as she continued.

"But it happens to have a larger than normal lens that I think will work perfectly for what you described."

When she removed the unit from the box Luke was immediately satisfied. The lens was easily four inches in diameter and could fit completely over the end of the Ocular.

"That looks like what I need," Luke remarked.
 "What kind of video tape does it use?"
" More outdated stuff. Normal VHS," she told him.
"Very good. I'll take it. By the way, would you happen to have any duct tape?"

જ

Chapter Ten

From the taxi, Luke watched with apprehension as a small crowd had gathered outside of Samiha's place of residence. Scores of police had made their way through her front doors and were dragging her away.

Joseph, his hands bound behind his back, was bleeding badly from a severe gash on his forehead, was also being pulled and pushed into a waiting police van.

Commands from the authorities to have the crowds disperse had people running in all directions as the van pulled away with his two friends. Luke directed the driver to take him to the nearest Marriott Hotel.

Once settled in his room Luke called a friend and associate at the University in Chicago . It was several minutes before the operator could connect him. When he finally reached him Luke was shouting into the phone, as he relayed the details of the events of the past day.

"Get hold of the Administrator and tell him what's going on with me. Have him contact our friends at the embassy and put some really tough pressure on. Have them get an attorney over there for Samiha and her project manager. I'll be back here in two hours for your call back to me."

He paused to listen to his friend as he asked him questions.
"I can't go into detail right now, Jess," he explained.
"Just trust me. Nothing to date has ever been unearthed that can even come close to the discovery Samiha and her crew dug up .We suspect that the authorities here may have had something to do with the death of one of her workers, and right now there's no telling what they'll do next.

"Also, and this is very important, I want you to book two reservations for Samiha and myself for the day after tomorrow's return to the States. By reserving the seats from there, they won't be noticed until we're long gone.

"Get on this right now! Hurry! Call me back in two hours."

As soon as he hung up he went right to work connecting the Ocular with the new camcorder.

Luke strolled out of the hotel looking like a typical nerdy tourist. The knee length shorts he'd purchased were plaid checkered and the Hawaiian multi-colored shirt and leather sandals completed his disguise. Over his shoulder he carried the overnight bag containing the Ocular now connected with duct tape to the camcorder. The only attention he attracted was accompanied by several occasional discrete snickers from a local passer by.

He hailed a taxi and directed him to drive into the general area of the police compound, where his friends were being held. He had the driver pull over a little distance away from the building, paid him and sent him on his way. He selected an outdoor tavern that was situated close enough to the police building to allow an unobstructed view, but far enough away to maintain safe distance while he watched the entrance.

Then he took a seat at one of the tables and ordered a beer. From out of his wallet he retrieved the needle, then removed the duct taped contraption that only served to accent his nerdy tourist appearance. No one gave him a second glance as he raised it to his level of vision and began to scan the front of the police compound. He gently traced the bottom of the Ocular with the needle until he was satisfied with his settings, then held it motionless for a moment. He was slightly startled by what he was able to see.

Less than an hour earlier the police van had pulled up to the entrance and unloaded its newest occupants, Joseph and Samiha. Luke had to look up from the machine and out at the present image to reassure himself that he was looking into the past.

Again, he raised the Ocular's eyepiece to his sights and watched. The van was greeted by a host of uniformed police and one civilian official who appeared to be in command. Luke took special notice of him. He did not look like a local, with the light skin of a European and dressed in an expensive suit that was definitely out of character for the neighborhood.

He re-ran the sequence several times, then moved the needle even farther along the base of the Ocular until he came to the time he was searching for. Much earlier in the day, another police van had dropped off the young boy who was also ushered into the building, bound and dragged, his face and arms bloodied and bruised from the markings of a beating. After watching the scene for a while Luke saw that it was some time before the European official arrived, pulling up in his own luxury sports sedan, and Luke surmised, well after the boy had already been killed.

He set the Ocular down on the table and sipped his beer while thinking of what to do next. He decided to retrace the movements of the official and find out where he'd come from, hoping that in doing so, other clues the identity of the European looking official might come to light.

Luke checked the time on his wrist watch, then returned the Ocular to the bag and waived down another taxi. He directed the driver to head out toward the main highway that lead north, and where the official had come from.

"Ya'll got some pretty gal dang nice country out here," Luke broke into a mock Texas drawl with the driver, with the idea to maintain the tourist image as convincingly as he could.

"Ya mind just taking up the highway there so's I kin get some pichers of this beautiful countryside?"

His chauffer calmly nodded without a word, in tolerant compliance and headed out into the direction Luke indicated. The highway stretched for miles in a straight line, with no exits or cut offs for as far as the eye could see. They drove for almost fifteen minutes before a road sign loomed up ahead, indicating a fork in the path. Luke waited until they were almost upon it when he asked the driver to pull over to the side. Then he loaded a blank VHS tape into the recorder.

"Hang here a second buddy. I'm gonna get a couple pictures."

Luke removed the Ocular and rested atop the taxi's roof and leaned over it to peer through the viewfinder. He made his adjustments with the needle by feeling along the base of the machine, as he scanned the two possible directions in which the sports sedan could have come from, hours earlier. Soon he saw that the official had originated from a cut off to the east. Satisfied, he loaded the Ocular back into the bag and got back into the taxi.

"Sure is purdy out here," he remarked.
"Just keep going down thisaway for a spell," he told the driver. Luke realized that the road they were now taking lead in the direction of the general area of Samiha's dig site, which was another ten or fifteen miles farther. His suspicions were confirmed when after another quarter hour of driving they came to the top of large hill and yet another fork in the road. Again, Luke ordered the driver to pull over.

Using the Ocular again to focus in on where the sedan had come from, Luke scanned the road ahead and the one less traveled path that led straight to the excavation site. He took his time tuning into the terrain below, at the base of the large hill, and very soon he was able to make out the image of the official's car. It had been parked very near to the site, among several other parked police vehicles. In the distance he could see the official as he walked with four uniformed police, stopping periodically to question several of the workers.

Luke was now convinced that the official, whoever he was, played a key role in the investigation of Samiha's discovery.

Luke continued to watch him as he mingled with the police and stopped periodically to investigate different areas of the site, and question the workers. After a while, he stopped recording the scene and returned the needle to his wallet. Then he slumped back into the seat of his taxi.

"By God, all this sight seein' got me plum tuckered out! Take me to my hotel, OK?"

&

Chapter Eleven

"Why are you keeping us here?" Samiha screamed at her captors. "We have committed no crime!"

Un-handcuffed now, Joseph sat quietly next to her as he dabbed at the gash in his forehead with a wet towel. Three police guards stood around them as one suited official paced the floor in front of them.

"You know the policy regarding the discovery of artifacts in this region," he began.
 "You're quite aware that all foreign expedition enterprises report immediately, anything and every-thing found to the authorities. We received word that you found something very out of the ordinary, and possibly of great value."

Samiha glared at him with contempt in her eyes.

"We found a lot of things," she blurted.
 "And the only thing out of the ordinary was a strange scrap of masonry carving that I would have gladly shared with you, if your goons hadn't been so preoccupied with beating my assistant!"
"That's all you found?" he asked.
"That's all!" she lied.
"That's not what we heard," he retorted.
"To hell with what you heard!" She screamed.

An urgent knock at the door interrupted the questioning. Another suited official entered the room and motioned his associate to follow him.

Out of ear shot in an adjacent room the two spoke together.

"Howard, with the boy dead and no collaboration, we have nothing. Besides, they found no evidence at her home, and to make matters worse, I just got a call from the embassy. Their sending down an attorney right now. Who knows? Maybe these friends of the kid were just fabricating a story. We can't risk an international incident right now over the words of some kids. "Clean them up, and when their attorney arrives, let them go. Smooth this over and make our apologies. Do whatever you have to do to appease them for now. It appears they have big friends in high places. But then, just keep an eye on them."

"Are you sure about this?" the other asked.
"Just do it," he replied.
 "Where can they go? If they have something we should know about, we'll get it soon enough."
"I'll submit an initial report to the big guys in Tel Aviv and if they decide to proceed further I'll ask them what next steps to take. If they tell us to go to the next level of investigation we'll know what to do and take it from there."

The conversation between the two white robed comrades continued well into the evening.

"These Earthly brethren of ours have another term, coined by one of their most honored and respected teachers of psychology. A man called Doctor Sigmund Freud. The term they use is ego. "This ego, or false personality, dominates almost all of their thought process. And what is this ego?

"The ego is idolatry; the sign of limited and separated self, born in a body, doomed to suffer and to end its life in death. It is the will that sees the Will of *Source* as enemy, and takes a form in which It is denied.

"The ego is the "proof" that strength is weak and love is fearful, life is really death, and what opposes *Source* alone is true. The ego is insane. In fear it stands beyond the Everywhere, apart from All, in separation from the Infinite.

"In its insanity it thinks it has become a victor over *Source* Itself, and in its terrible autonomy it "sees" the Will of *Source* has been destroyed. It dreams of punishment, and trembles at the figures in its dreams, its enemies who seek to murder it before it can ensure its safety by attacking them.

"The children of the *Source* is egoless. What can they know of madness and the death of *Source*, when he abides in Him? What can he know of sorrow and of suffering, when he lives in eternal joy? What can he know of fear and punishment, of sin and guilt, of hatred and attack, when all there is surrounding him is everlasting peace, forever conflict-free and undisturbed, in deepest silence and tranquility?

To know Reality is not to see the ego and its thoughts, its works, its acts, its laws and its beliefs, its dreams, its hopes, its plans for its salvation, and the cost belief in it entails. In suffering, the price for faith in it is so immense that crucifixion of the children of *Source* is offered daily at its darkened shrine, and blood must flow before the altar where its sickly followers prepare for death.

Yet will one lily of forgiveness change the darkness into light; the altar to illusions to the shrine of Life Itself. And peace will be restored forever to the holy minds which *Source* created as His Son, His dwelling-place, His joy, His love, completely His, completely one with Him."

"And this "sin" you refer to," the younger of the two began, "is the perception of attack upon that which the ego cherishes?"
"Exactly!" The elder replied, and he continued,
"Sin is insanity. It is the means by which the mind is driven mad, and seeks to let illusions take the place of truth. And being mad, it sees illusions where truth should be, and where it really is. Sin

gave the body eyes, for what is there the sinless would behold? What need have they of sights or sounds or touch? What would they hear or reach to grasp? What would they sense at all?

"*To sense is not to know.* And truth can be but filled with knowledge, and with nothing else. The body is the instrument the mind made in its striving to deceive itself. Its purpose is to strive. Yet can the goal of striving change. And now the body serves a different aim for striving. What it seeks for now is chosen by the aim the mind has taken as replacement for the goal of self-deception. Truth can be its aim as well as lies. The senses then will seek instead for witnesses to what is true.

"Sin is the home of all illusions, which but stand for things imagined, issuing from thoughts which are untrue. They are the "proof" that what has no reality is real. Sin "proves" *Source's* Son is evil; timelessness must have an end; Eternal life must die. And *Source* Himself has lost the Son He loves, with but corruption to complete Himself, His Will forever overcome by death, love slain by hate, and peace to be no more.

"A madman's dreams are frightening, and sin appears indeed to terrify. And yet what sin perceives is but a childish game. The Son of *Source* may play he has become a body, prey to evil and to guilt, with but a little life that ends in death. But all the while his Father shines on him, and loves him with an everlasting Love which his pretenses cannot change at all.

"There is no sin. Creation is unchanged."

෴

Chapter Twelve

Luke stopped at the hotel's main desk to check for messages,
then rushed back to his room when he was informed that there
were none. He removed VHS tape recording and loaded it into
the unit above his TV, then reviewed the sequence of events he
had just filmed.

He was studying every frame when the phone rang. It was his
friend and colleague, Jess. He relayed the details of the confirmed
reservation for two on the day after tomorrow's morning's flight,
and that an attorney for the administration was on his way to the
police station to secure the release of Samiha and Joseph even as
they spoke.

"Good job," Luke told him.
 "I'll get down there and meet the attorney right now. Watch for
me in a couple of days. Thanks, Jess!"

Luke changed into dress slacks and a sport jacket, then gathered
up the Ocular and video cam and loaded everything back into his
overnight bag. At the front desk he had the bag secured into the
hotel safe, before requesting another taxi.
In the lobby of the police compound a small thin man greeted
Luke.
 "Are you Luke Ozman?"
"I am."
"Hiemie Wienstien," the man introduced himself with his out
stretched hand.
"I'm the attorney assigned to help with this situation. I represent
several friendly embassy concerns in the area, and I must say,
I'm very impressed. You have some very influential friends!
"The local authorities have been instructed to release your two
co-workers."
"How long will that take?" Luke asked him.
"They're on their way up now," he assured him.

A man emerged from an office at the end of the lobby and headed straight for Luke and the attorney. Luke recognized him immediately as the European official he'd tracked and recorded earlier.

He extended his hand to Luke and introduced himself. It was like shaking the surface skin of a cold limp catfish. Luke disguised his contempt.

"Howard Frazes, at your service, sir. May I ask, what is your connection with the two people we have in custody?"
"They work for me as subcontractors on an archeological expedition sponsored by Loyola University in Chicago , Illinois , USA . They're part of our team."

"Interesting," Frazes acknowledged. He then motioned to a guard that stood outside of the door from which he'd emerged and immediately Samiha and Joseph entered the lobby.

Luke ran to Samiha and took her into his arms. She fell into his embrace and sobbed quietly. Joseph joined them, and Luke reached out to hug him. The three of them held one another for a while before Frazes interrupted them.

"We apologize for the inconvenience you have endured, but you must understand, it's important for us to keep a close scrutiny upon all digs of this kind. We try to minimize the possibility of foreign theft and destruction of this region's ancient artifacts and historically valuable sites. Our policies seem strict but necessary."

Luke glared at him, then at the wound on Joseph's forehead.

"Do your policies always include beating innocent people?"
Frazes shook his head and looked away.
"Again, we apologize. The police may have been overly aggressive."

Wienstien nodded to Frazes, thanked him, then ushered the three friends out of the building. Outside on the steps, Luke thanked the attorney.

"I'll give you all a lift home," Weinstien offered.
"Thanks," Luke acknowledged. "If you don't mind, we need to take a detour past the Marriott. I need to pick up my overnight bag."

Joseph wore a fresh bandage, protecting the wound on his forehead that covered his recent injury and rested in a chair on the balcony across from Samiha and Luke who sat at the table together.

Luke had cautioned them about saying anything related to the Ocular in the apartment, just for the possibility that an electronic bug may have been planted when the authorities searched the place earlier.

Samiha was still very upset by the ordeal at the police station and occasionally wiped a fresh tear from her eyes.
"Don't worry," Luke told her as he held her hand and patted it comfortingly.

"You and I are getting out of here the day after tomorrow."
Samiha leaned over and kissed him on the lips.
"Thank you Luke. I don't know what we'd do if you weren't here."
"When we're safely back in the States, I'm gonna raise a stink about this!" Luke went on.
"These bastards aren't getting away with what they did to that poor boy or for roughing up you two."
Samiha studied his face and smiled at him.

"I'm glad you're on my side," she told him and leaned over to kiss him once again, then continued.

"Why have you never married, Luke?"

Luke paused and just looked at her, unprepared for her question. "I don't know. I suppose I just never found the right person. Maybe it's not something high in priority with me. Besides, you know how I feel about man-made tradition. One doesn't need the consecration of an artificial ceremony or official documents to establish love.

"Why haven't *you*?" he retorted.
She continued to smile at him, then looked up at the early evening sky and the stars that had begun to twinkle to life. "My religion wouldn't approve of my love," she said quietly. Luke looked at her with new interest. They'd always shared a brief, but distinct attraction for one another that had not diminished over the years.

"What does religion have to do with love?' Luke asked her and he continued.
"One of the greatest spiritual minds of our time writes about it when he says, that the human emotional system can be broken down roughly into two elements: fear and love. He explains how fear is of the personality, what we learn, not what we're born with. Love is of the soul, and souls have no specific religion, color, nationality or creed. All negativity comes from the personality and all love comes from the soul."

Samiha squirmed uncomfortably.
"I'm very familiar with your ideas on religion, Luke. And although I respect your values and opinions, the fact remains that I was taught some very strict guidelines with regard to my own spirituality. These are important to me, and I must adhere to them."
them or what? You'll go to hell if you don't?" Luke persisted.

She jerked her head in his direction, but said nothing. He went on.

"What if I told you that there was no hell, that the idea of a place of punishment like that was created by personalities with the intention to instill fear and guilt and keep followers in line?"

"You can't be serious," Samiha blurted.

Luke shrugged his shoulders.

"You're a scientist Samiha. Think about it. If a spaceship landed on the White House lawn tomorrow, what religion would its occupants be?"

"Luke, you're touching on grounds that have been long ago established in deep religious tradition."

"Yes, but just how long ago?" he retorted.

"Who set the ground rules? For what reasons? Do you really believe that the God of one religion is any different than the God of another? Would a God of the magnitude we attest to, separate one man from another, choose who would be *better* or *worse*, or more *right* or *wrong* than any other? Who would be more pleasing in *His* eyes?

"Religions tend to ascribe to their specific God, characteristics found in man, yet the longer I live, the more convinced I am of the fact that first, we're not alone in the universe, and second, we're most probably a part of a common population of a much bigger universal family whose existence is comprised of a special group of beings that are capable of evolution, in every sense of the word.

"I believe that *God* is the universal power that binds and connects everything and everyone, and that we occupy this tiny fragment of creation called Earth still thinking that everything revolves around it. Earth-bound tradition can't see the forest for the trees while we live our lives struggling to pay the rent or worrying about who's gonna win the World Series.

"We fear anything we don't understand, and create mythical fairy tales to satisfy our own justification for a lack of effort to really try to investigate and comprehend the truth."

They were silent for a long time. Joseph was smiling at Luke, and nodding his head but saying nothing.
Luke rambled on.
"Religions created witch hunts and murdered so called heretics, like researchers who studied the possibility that the Earth wasn't really flat. Some popular religions teach to this very day, that God was in the real estate business and delegated certain tracts of land to certain groups of people. Others twist and distort scriptures to fit their own purposes."

Samiha move her face closer to Luke's and looked deeply into his eyes.

"You're one very intelligent bastard," she said, then laughed.
Luke laughed with her and leaned closer to kiss her on the cheek.
"I just find it very discouraging that every single organized religion on Earth festers with in insatiable need to argue their own points of view, even to the degree of taking it to all out violent confrontation. Man created religions, not God."
He allowed the thought to linger for a moment then changed the subject.

"I wanted to tell you," he began, "before we received the horrible news of what happened to your young digger, that while I was out today, I did a little investigation of my own with the Ocular. I was experimenting with it and the first place I visited was the site of the excavation and I found out some very interesting things."
"Like what?" Samiha asked.

"I confirmed some old suspicions for some of the reasons why the pyramids were built and who influenced their construction."
"Your kidding!" Samiha exclaimed. "Go on!"

Luke continued. "For a few hours I used the ocular to help
confirm or better explain some of the theories and beliefs many
scientists hold with regard to the reasoning that went into their
construction. What I discovered was remarkable to say the least.
Bear with me a bit.

"We know, as archeologists, that there are some strange
coincidences that connect the Great Pyramid and those in the
region, with other pyramids built all over the world. For instance,
we know that the base dimensions of the Great Pyramid at Giza
are almost exactly identical to those of The Pyramid of the Sun in
Mexico City . We know that there are startling similarities in both
designs, and the strangeness doesn't end there.

"We also know that a stark connection with the alignment of the
constellation Orion, also coincides with distinct features built into
the Great Pyramid and that the three largest structures line up
almost within a pins head of precise relation to one another.
"We know other things too. We know about how close each giant
stone was set next to each other, some so perfectly that it's
difficult if not impossible to detect any separation at all.
"But until now, we really know very little about its actual
builders, nor are we certain of what technology was used to
design it."

"So what did you find?" Judy asked him.

"What I discovered," Luke went on, "confirmed some of my own
suspicions. And this Time Ocular proves things without a chance
for error. I found that intelligence of a major technological scale
has been around a lot longer than we have thus far believed. And
although we have come very far in our own era of technological
advancement, the truth is, we're only following a path that has
already been traveled, perhaps many times before."

"That possibility has always occurred to me." Samiha stated.
Luke went on.

"Yes, but what I found would literally shake the entire foundation of everything we have assumed, or theorized or labeled as so called history."

He paused a moment and looked up at the night sky before continuing.

"I saw the man who buried the Ocular."

Joseph and Samiha looked at him with new interest.

"You actually saw him?" Samiha asked.

Luke nodded.

"I watched him as he placed it into a newly trenched footing that was dug to accommodate the door jam. And, I saw the original surroundings of an active community of laborers. You were quite correct in your evaluation of the purpose for why the city was constructed. It *is* the remains of the living quarters and residences of the people who built it. And I saw other things."

"What?" Samiha urged.

Luke took several deep breaths before looking into her eyes and continuing.

"You know, I never gave much credibility to the content of supermarket tabloids, but what I'm about to tell you, I hafta admit, seems even more strange than any of the articles ever printed in those things. If I hadn't seen it with my own eyes, I certainly would never believe it.

"I tuned in to the time when the machine was buried, saw who planted it there, then fast forwarded the scene over many centuries. I was looking for a change in the behavior of the residents. And then I found it.

"A dark blotch appeared in the viewfinder and seemed to last a very long time, so I went back to the point where the darkness began and calculated that several hundred years after the pyramid was built something terrible went on in the area. I focused in on a particular day and saw a flurry of uncommon activity among the residents of the community.

Everyone was scurrying about in hurry and it became apparent that a general alarm of some kind had been proclaimed throughout the area. I watched as hundreds and hundreds of people filed into a base entrance of the pyramid, all carrying items of personal property. Food, animals, tools and stores that one would expect to take along for simple survival. I scanned the scene forward for a few days and until there was no more movement going on, and it appeared that everyone had settled into the shelter of the pyramid. The entire place became totally deserted.

"Then I saw why. As I scanned the horizon I discovered something that took my breath away. It was an enormous ball of fire that came from the western sky and passed very closely overhead, then crashed into the ground with such fury that everything went dark. I realized that what I had just witnessed was an asteroid, a very large one, that had slammed into their neighborhood only a few miles to the east.

"I scrolled forward for what I determined to be several years until the light gradually returned, and slowly and gradually I could once again make out distinctive shapes and images. Eventually I was able to see the top half of the pyramid. Dirt, soot and debris of all kinds had cluttered the base, and now ice completely covered the surface of the pyramid. What had once been an area of green pastures and colorful terrain was now rocky, and desolate. There were no trees left, and as far as I could see, no running water.

"I moved the needle ever so slightly to speed up the sequence and soon came to the time when the full light of the Sun returned. The ice that had blanketed the surface of the pyramid was melting rapidly and before too long I started to see movement on a particular spot near the top.

"I saw stones being moved and tumbling down the side and then I saw the people as they emerged, one by one, until a small gathering of survivors made their way to the ground. And then I understood that these beings foretold what had happened, expected it, and were quite prepared to deal with it."

Samiha and Joseph were awe stricken as they listened attentively to Luke's account. He went on.

"They knew in advance that the asteroid was due to hit.
"I always suspected that there were bigger and better reasons for why the pyramids were built, and that although in the thousands of generations of their existence, they may well have been converted to tombs and burial places for kings, I think that the original plan was for protection against an impending disaster that they knew was coming. I believe that the intricate design of the interior was specifically created to house and separate, and to enable avenues of escape when the time came.

"They brought their food and animals to live on, their personal possessions, probably their gold and obviously many of their tools. They sought shelter in a place that provided a degree of protection not available anywhere else in the immediate region."

"At the risk of sounding too stupid," Samiha began, "are you saying that the pyramids were originally used as a kind of bomb shelter?"

"That's precisely what I'm saying," Luke replied and he continued,
"We've always made out assumptive evaluations of the pyramids based on the *final* entries, the remains of what went on thousands of years *after* this major calamity. What I saw with my own eyes is what occurred early in its life not long after it was built. The discoveries contemporary archeologists made of items found were probably not things one would normally take to a grave, or with its occupants as they traveled over some border to a mythical place between here and the hereafter. They were things ordinary people needed to survive."

Joseph continued to watch Luke and listen carefully to every word, while he remained silently mesmerized by everything he heard.

"The fact is, whatever we know about the pyramids and their history is so far removed from the truth that we may as well have just stumbled onto them yesterday. Modern, so called historians, typically tainted the truth with subjective theory mixed with their own convenient accounts which always lent to traditional religious ideology. They force fed the young minds eager to learn, with a lot of crap."

"Luke!" Samiha called out to him harshly.
"Aren't you being a little too judgmental? Not everything all historians say is crap!"
Luke paused for a moment and looked at her.

"Maybe not," he admitted,
"But people have been hoodwinked and lied to all too much. They're forced to accept explanations of events that only enhance the opinions of the powers that be at the time. I'm sick of it! The Earth is not the center of the Universe and the sooner that fact is realized the closer to truth will we all become. The closer will everyone come to the realization that we are all one, one race, one spirituality, one humanity.

"I made the example of the space ship landing on the White House lawn for one reason; we attribute to ourselves things that are not our possessions. We think that we own the Earth. We think that we're separate from everything else, including some of our own kind and we believe that we're unique. But the shuddering fact remains that we are not. And worst of all, we fight among ourselves to the point of all out war, just to defend who's right, when always, without exception, both sides, like the Hatfields and McCoys, are equally wrong and equally right."
Samiha let out a long sigh.
"You need to get some rest, Luke. It's getting late."

He relaxed and nodded in agreement. Then he said,
"Tomorrow morning I want you to have your surveyor team meet
us here. Have them bring several tripods and lots of equipment. If
we're being watched, the Ocular will blend right in as part of the
team's equipment."

"What do you want to do at the site tomorrow?" Samiha asked
him.
"I want to trace the movements of the man who buried the
machine there and get an idea, if possible, how it came into his
possession."

ʠ

Chapter Thirteen

The moon loomed full in the night sky as the two friends
continued to share conversation.
The younger posed a question.

"You mentioned the fact that some of our earthly brethren, a
small number of them, have achieved a degree of conscious
understanding. Can you say that among these a few teachers of
truth and *Source* that they can help the rest of them? And can it
be that these teachers have the ability to lead and guide their
brothers to greater understanding? "

"You can indeed!" The elder replied.
"In fact their history is rich with accounts of such teachers who
lived, taught and prospered in all areas of this planet, from
remote islands to the great plains of the western continent and all
throughout the east.

"One common characteristic among these teachers of the *Source*
is Trust.
"This *trust* is the foundation on which their ability to fulfill their
function rests. Perception is the result of learning. In fact,
perception *is* learning, because cause and effect are never
separated. The teachers of *Source* have trust in the world, because
they have learned it is not governed by the laws the world made
up. It is governed by a Power That is *in* them but not *of* them. It is
this Power That keeps all things safe. It is through this Power that
the teachers of *Source* look on a forgiven world.

"When this Power has once been experienced, it is impossible to
trust one's own petty strength again. Who would attempt to fly
with the tiny wings of a sparrow when the mighty power of an
eagle has been given him? And who would place his faith in the
shabby offerings of the ego when the gifts of *Source* are laid
before him? What is it that induces them to make the shift?

"First, they must go through what might be called "a period of undoing."

This need not be painful, but it usually is so experienced. It seems as if things are being taken away, and it is rarely understood initially that their lack of value is merely being recognized. How can lack of value be perceived unless the perceiver is in a position where he must see things in a different light? He is not yet at a point at which he can make the shift entirely internally. And so the plan will sometimes call for changes in what seem to be external circumstances. These changes are always helpful. When the teacher of *Source* has learned that much, he goes on to the second stage.

"Next, the teacher of *Source* must go through "a period of sorting out." This is always somewhat difficult because, having learned that the changes in his life are always helpful, he must now decide all things on the basis of whether they increase the helpfulness or hamper it. He will find that many, if not most of the things he valued before will merely hinder his ability to transfer what he has learned to new situations as they arise.

Because he has valued what is really valueless, he will not generalize the lesson for fear of loss and sacrifice. It takes great learning to understand that all things, events, encounters and circumstances are helpful. It is only to the extent to which they are helpful that any degree of reality should be accorded them in this world of illusion. The word "value" can apply to nothing else.

"The third stage through which the teacher of *Source* must go can be called "a period of relinquishment." If this is interpreted as giving up the desirable, it will engender enormous conflict. Few teachers of *Source* escape this distress entirely. There is, however, no point in sorting out the valuable from the valueless unless the next obvious step is taken. Therefore, the period of overlap is apt to be one in which the teacher of *Source* feels called upon to sacrifice his own best interests on behalf of truth.

He has not realized as yet how wholly impossible such a demand would be. He can learn this only as he actually does give up the valueless. Through this, he learns that where he anticipated grief, he finds a happy lightheartedness instead; where he thought something was asked of him, he finds a gift bestowed on him.

"Now comes "a period of settling down." This is a quiet time, in which the teacher of *Source* rests a while in reasonable peace. Now he consolidates his learning. Now he begins to see the transfer value of what he has learned. Its potential is literally staggering, and the teacher of *Source* is now at the point in his progress at which he sees in it his whole way out.
 "Give up what you do not want, and keep what you do."

"How simple is the obvious! And how easy to do! The teacher of *Source* needs this period of respite. He has not yet come as far as he thinks. Yet when he is ready to go on, he goes with mighty companions beside him. Now he rests a while, and gathers them before going on. He will not go on from here alone.

"The next stage is indeed "a period of unsettling." Now must the teacher of *Source* understand that he did not really know what was valuable and what was valueless. All that he really learned so far was that he did not want the valueless, and that he did want the valuable. Yet his own sorting out was meaningless in teaching him the difference. The idea of sacrifice, so central to his own thought system, had made it impossible for him to judge.

"He thought he learned willingness, but now he sees that he does not know what the willingness is for. And now he must attain a state that may remain impossible to reach for a long, long time. He must learn to lay all judgment aside, and ask only what he really wants in every circumstance. Were not each step in this direction so heavily reinforced, it would be hard indeed!

"And finally, there is "a period of achievement." It is here that learning is consolidated. Now what was seen as merely shadows before become solid gains, to be counted on in all "emergencies" as well as tranquil times. Indeed, the tranquility is their result; the outcome of honest learning, consistency of thought and full transfer. This is the stage of real peace, for here is Ultimate Peace's state fully reflected. From here, the way to Ultimate Peace's is open and easy. In fact, it is here. Who would "go" anywhere, if peace of mind is already complete? And who would seek to change tranquility for something more desirable? What could be more desirable than this?"

Chapter Fourteen

The following morning they all rose early. Out front of the residence, they met a battered old pick-up truck manned by three members of Samiha's crew, all assigned to the duties of surveying. The bed of the vehicle was loaded with tripods, and scopes of varying sizes.

Luke scrambled aboard the rear and helped Samiha and Joseph climb in then signaled the driver to head to the site. Luke retrieved a blank video cartridge from his overnight bag and inserted it into the camcorder.

Once they arrived at the dig Samiha directed her crew to park just above the location that overlooked the spot where the Ocular was found, then had her men prepare to check the exact distances of the width and length of perimeter of the site.

"I gave them something to do," Samiha explained to Luke. "It'll keep them occupied for a while and not appearing too suspicious while you're busy."

Joseph motioned for them to look at a car that was parked about two hundred yards away in the distance.

"We have company," he announced.
Two suited men sat motionless in the car, observing them, each with a pair of binoculars.

"Keep a discreet eye on them, Joseph," Luke told him. "If they stay there, we'll be alright. If they look like they start to head this way, we'll pack up and leave." Then he took one of the tripods and set it up on the ground directly over the position he needed to acquire a view of the door jam. Samiha stood next him, as he placed the Ocular atop the tripod and focused in on the dig area and the hole that had been created when the Ocular was discovered.

With the needle, he touched the base of the Ocular then began to move it forward very slightly until he came to the moment in time he was looking for. He paused then, and studied the scene for a few minutes, while the recorder ran.

"Here. Take a look," Luke instructed Samiha.
She peered through the viewfinder and was immediately surprised.
 "My God!" she exclaimed.
 "I see him."

She observed a young man, whose age she determined to be somewhere in his mid-thirties, dressed in a full length of white robes, as he knelt at the doorway and buried the Ocular before covering the opening he'd created with the wood base of the door jam. When he was finished, he stood up and looked around the area. He was tall, with features that seemed to be mixed with those of local nationality, but darker skin and eyes that sharpened slightly at the corners. His hair flowed long past his shoulders. Samiha motioned for Joseph to look.

After a few minutes Luke took control of the Ocular over again.
"He's moving away now," Luke told them.
"Stay with me. I'm gonna follow where he goes."

Joseph helped with the tripod by lifting it gently as Luke held it from the top and scanned the area below slowly.

"This way," he directed.
Keeping his eyes glued to the viewfinder, Luke walked away from the site and headed toward the outer ridge and away from all of the work activity. His friends stayed with him until he stopped at a spot about fifty yards up the hill near a slightly grassy area.

He continued to stare through the eyepiece, his mouth slightly opened in amazement, and very engrossed in what he was looking at. After a short while he looked up from the machine and over at Samiha. His eyes were wide with astonishment.

"What is it Luke?" she whispered.
"He's led us purposely to this place. He knew that someone would find it and now the man is motioning through time, as if inviting us."

Luke waved for Samiha to move closer and share the view, allowing her to look with her left eye, while he used his right, and, cheek to cheek, study the scene together.
The young man sat cross-legged outside of an open-air tent where he held his arms up in a gesture of invitation.

"Look at the rug that's laid out in from of him," Luke directed her. The young man was seated near one edge of a large, beautifully woven carpet that had been decorated with intricate images and colorful designs. Near the center of the rug was an elaborate depiction of what appeared to be a map of the earth that covered over five square feet of its area. Beneath the map was a more familiar work of art. It was a painting in exact detail of the stone carving of the planets they had recently discovered.

Luke and Samiha watched as the man used a finger of his right hand to point at the fourth planet from the Sun, then he slowly raised his hand and with the same finger, touched his chest. He then looked up from the image below him, out at his future guests, and smiled.

Samiha gasped in awe.
"He's telling us that he's from Mars!" she exclaimed.
"Yes he is," Luke acknowledged reverently.

The three of them remained there for another few minutes as Luke continued to record the event, and occasionally allowed Joseph to get a look at what they were watching. The two men in

the distance hadn't moved but Luke decided that he didn't want
to stay any longer.

"Let's pack this all up and go back to your place before our
watchdogs get any ideas about taking a stroll over here."
Back at her residence, Luke played the recording several times,
studying every detail as they talked about it.

"There's no dispute among the scientific world that Mars endured
a great, global scale calamity," Luke was saying.

"Neither is there any longer, doubt within the community of
researchers that Mars was once teaming with oceans, rivers and
vegetation. Too much proof from the fly bys of the Mariner probe
and the new discoveries by recent Spirit and Opportunity rover
landings substantiates that fact. And now we know from the
images on the carving and on that carpet that the comet that
slammed into Jupiter and created Venus, was the reason for why
Mars is in the condition it is today."

Samiha nodded.
 "And some of the survivors made it here to Earth!" she
commented.
"That appears to be true," Luke agreed.
 "But exactly how long ago, and what important influences those
survivors had on their new earthly frontier, remains to be seen.
One thing is certain now. More creditability can now be
established for the existence of artificial constructions and
pyramids on Mars."

"What artificial constructions, Luke?" Joseph asked him.
"You're not aware of those things?"
"No," Joseph replied. "What are you referring to?"

Luke smiled at him while inwardly curious at his lack of
knowledge on these facts. He continued with his explanation.

"It seems that NASA's Mariner, launched in the mid seventies, programmed to map the surface of Mars, took some pretty eye brow raising photographs of an area they coined Cydonia.

"Cydonia appears to be the remains of a community that once thrived on the banks of a great body of water, and is dotted with very distinct images of five-sided pyramids and a human face, carved from stone, that stares straight out into the heavens." Joseph's mouth dropped open in astonishment.
 "I wasn't aware of that!"

Luke nodded understandingly. He went on.
"Don't feel rained on. Many people don't know about it. In fact it wasn't until years after the photos were taken, before some inquiring minds looked into it and forced NASA to come clean about what they found. And as always is the case with discoveries of phenomena of this kind, it was explained away as nonsense or optical illusions or natural forms created by winds. Typical rebuttals are always covered up with claims that they are not pyramids at all and the face is just an interpretation of the ravings of UFO buffs or cultists."

"But how could a discovery of this magnitude be kept from the public?" Joseph wailed.
Luke shook his head.
"It's like anything else. It works on the Big Lie theory. The bigger the lie the more believe it. Like Oswald firing the magic bullet.
"Most people don't want to know the truth or would rather allow others to think for them, than investigate for themselves." He moved over to the table where the Ocular lay and gently patted it. "Let's see if they call this weather balloons, swamp gas or an optical illusion."

"What are your plans, Luke?"
"Well," he began, "We already have enough video footage on VCR tape that will raise a few more eye brows. So our next move will be to get back to the States, and around our people at the

University. People we can trust and who'll help us. There are too many eyes on us here."

&

The next morning the three friends rose very early. After showering and packing the remaining few items for their trip, Luke checked his watch for the time and gave some last minute instructions to Joseph.
"Use Samiha's vehicle and take your time driving over to the dig site. Stop somewhere along the way and get some coffee or something. If anyone is watching us this early, it'll split them up."

Luke grabbed his shoulders in a friendly embrace.
"It's certain now that we're being watched very closely. Samiha and I will slip out through the fields in the rear, and walk the mile to the airport. You take care of yourself, and if you need anything call the attorney."

Joseph nodded obediently, then hugged Luke before turning to Samiha. She smiled at him, and kissed him on the cheek. She spoke some reassuring words in Arabic then kissed him again. They watched through the window as Joseph left, then walked down the rear stairs to a rarely used exit that opened up to field of trees and shrubbery. Luke cautiously searched the horizon for any sign of suspicious observers, then satisfied, motioned for Samiha to follow as they scurried quickly through the thick cover, each of them wheeling a piece of light luggage behind them. Strapped to his right shoulder, Luke carried an overnight bag that contained the precious Ocular and tapes they'd recorded.

Samiha hiked briskly beside him, although slightly uncom-fortable in her present attire. Luke had instructed her to wear something revealing and attractive and she didn't disappoint him. Her short black skirt ended a full foot above her knees and the matching silk halter-top was barely adequate to contain her exceptionally endowed breasts, which spilled invitingly over the brief cleavage area.

"Why did you have me dress like this?" she whispered to him as they approached the airport terminal.
Luke smiled at her.
"Because beauty like yours is unapproachable, and right now I don't want anyone approaching us."

She returned his smile and winked at him seductively.
Samiha passed through the security gate while dozens of smiling eyes watched her, and Luke followed, loading their baggage onto the conveyor belt that would be scanned and x-rayed. One of the guards studied his screen curiously when the overnight bag reached the point of inspection. He pressed the stop button and examined it more closely, then motioned for one of his associate guards to remove the bag.

The two guards then opened it and peered inside while rummaging their hands through its contents.
Luke's heart leaped into his mouth but he kept his composure as they fondled the Ocular and the video camcorder.

"Video equipment?" one of them asked Luke.
He nodded an acknowledgement as Samiha leaned closer and smiled at the two guards.

"We made some home movies of me at the hotel swimming pool!" she announced as she winked at the officer.
Both guards grinned widely while staring at her breasts. They zipped the bag close and let it pass.

"Have a nice trip," one of them offered. Luke shouldered the bag again and smiled at them as they walked away toward the reservations desk.

As promised, their tickets were waiting and as they approached
their boarding gate Luke let out a sigh of relief.
"I almost soiled my pants back there," he whispered to her.
"I thought you were pretty cool about it," Samiha complimented.
Luke just rolled his eyes.
 "Well, the hard part is over." He glanced at his watch again.
"We'll be boarding any minute now."

At the headquarters for Mossad in Tel Aviv, Meir Gurion was
speaking quietly and with pronounced urgency to his associate,
David Yatom his highest ranking intelligence official. They were
discussing the contents of a recent dispatch from subordinate
operatives from the region of Giza .
Great concern was brewing among the top echelon at F.A.S. over
the discovery near the Great Pyramid, by Samiha's crew.

"Are you absolutely certain about the nature of what they
found?" Gurion asked the other.

"We are. There's no question about it." He replied, and went on,
"Our friends just completed an interview with one of the
principals closest to the actual event. Just minutes ago they
assured me, in no uncertain terms, that they are quite positive
about just what it was they unearthed."

Gurion muttered a Yiddish curse word then ran his hands across
his bald head in a movement of discouragement. He was
extremely irritated.

"How could this be?" He shouted angrily.

Yatom shrugged his shoulders. Although concerned, he wasn't as agitated as his associate.

"It appears that there were more than just one of those things laying around waiting to be dug up. It was always a possibility. We could never be completely confident in the idea that ours was the only one."

"Well, they must be stopped." Gurion snapped at him. "They cannot be allowed to keep it. We must do whatever we have to make sure of this!"

"It's already too late to intercept them on this side of the world." Yatom told him.

"My people informed me that the American and his Palestinian whore have already left the country and I have every reason to believe that the idiots at the airport's inspection terminal let them walk right through with the thing tucked in their carry-on on luggage."

Gurion sighed disgustedly, then paused to think for a moment before speaking again.
"Well then, our hands are forced to do what we must. Because, at all costs, the machine must not fall into the hands of the Americans. Do whatever you have to."
Yatom nodded.

"I understand," he acknowledged, then continued,
"I have four Metsada friends stationed very near where the archeologists are headed. I'll arrange for our friends to pay them a visit in their own city and deal with the matter there. We'll have that thing back here within twelve hours."
"See to it then." Gurion ordered then he added,
"These Metsada friends...You're positive they are the best suited and the most loyal for this?"

"They are." he assured him.

"I know of them personally and their record is impeccable. They have a one-hundred percent success history with issues like these in the past and they're very familiar with the USA territories, so they know their way around. And, they work privately, with no connection to any of our official resource programs."
"Good. Keep me updated."

&

Chapter Fifteen

The elder continued as they talked together well into the night.
"I realize that for you, my young friend, it may be a little difficult
to comprehend the gravity and the degree of these Earthly
brethren of ours complete and total ignorance of their
connectedness with *Source*. They don't have a clue. They're lost
in utter denial of the *Presence* of That Which sustains their very
existence.

"Their words and labels and definitions and positionalities all
stand in the way of Understanding."

His companion looked into the eyes of the elder.
"What do you mean, difficult for me to comprehend? I've
experienced many lifetimes, and most of which were immersed in
the same kinds of distractive separatist perception. I too spent
eons in dream state, unaware of *Source* and quite taken with the
illusion of form. And yes, all of those experiences exist only as a
passing dream in my recollection, but their remnants remain,
even if ever so faintly."
His older friend smiled.

"Of course."
And he went on.
"Tell me, please. What did you experience at the cusp of your
own moment of 'understanding?"

Now the younger one also smiled and answered immediately.
"That's easy. It was the experience of awakening from a deep
sleep. It was the underlying conviction that the end of dreams is
my heritage, guaranteed, because the Son of the *Source* can never
be abandoned. In Reality His dreams are gone and in their place
is the Truth established. "
His older friend cracked a wide grin.

They were silent for a long few minutes before the younger spoke again.

"With the discovery of the machines, our own history of the events that followed for many, many years, were the bleak and horrific times of discord, confusion and conflict. While it was the turning point in our own evolutionary understanding, it left in its wake much unrest and turmoil. Is this to be the fate of our friends here as well? Must they also endure the wrath of experience that accompanies new knowledge?"

"Unfortunately yes." The older one replied.
 ""What accompanies new knowledge, as you put it cannot be avoided. The very presence of discord is the golden link to their salvation. They must learn that there is no order of difficulty, no event or experience, either minor or seemingly too great to overcome, that can stand in their way if the means to perceive correctly are applied. And they will…eventually."

Chicago's O'Hare airport is one of the busiest in the entire world. Although their luggage was once again, checked and searched at the customs desk, the general atmosphere was much less tense, and everything went smoothly. Luke was obviously very happy to be back.

"I feel like kissing the ground!" he joked as they made their way out of the terminal and into the cool April air. He hailed the next taxi in line and the two of them settled comfortably into the rear passengers seat as it pulled away and headed for the city.

Luke lived in an apartment near Lake Michigan, and across from scenic Lincoln Park , not far from the city's main center of business. The taxi driver drove east on the Kennedy Expressway for about fifteen minutes then exited at Ohio street directly through the heart of downtown Chicago. Samiha's eyes were wide with delight as she took in the impressive sights of tall skyscrapers and the bustling activity of thousands of people, all moving as if they were in a great hurry.

"What a beautiful city!" she remarked as the cab turned south on LaSalle street, only a few blocks from Luke's home.

"One of the most beautiful in the world!" Luke responded.
The words were barely out of his mouth when suddenly, two loud gun shots rang out. The entire rear window of the cab came crashing in and Samiha screamed in horror. Luke instinctively grabbed her and threw her onto the floor, his body covering hers completely.

The driver slammed on his brakes, then wheeled the vehicle about in a one hundred eighty degree reverse as he quickly accelerated into the direction from which they come, weaving in and around on coming one-way traffic.

He sped furiously back down LaSalle street, then made a quick right turn onto a side street, disrupting traffic in his wake and sending several cars into uncontrollable collisions with one another.

"The shots came from a car right behind us," the driver shouted, as he speeded away from the melee of horns blasting and people shouting frantically behind them.
"Are you two alright?" he hollered.

Luke struggled back to his seat and helped Samiha who was visibly shaken with fear, as she clung to Luke in confused desperation.

"You're bleeding!" she exclaimed.
One of the bullets had grazed the left side of Luke's neck and left a thin red wound that he began to wipe with the sleeve of his jacket.

"Did you see who did the shooting?" Luke asked the driver.
The driver shook his head as he continued to widen the distance
between his taxi and the scene of the shooting.
 "All I saw was a dark car behind us moving up along our right
side, then I heard the shots."

Samiha nursed his wound with some tissue, still very nervous
while her eyes welled up with tears. She sobbed uncontrollably
while Luke struggled with trying to figure out who could have
been responsible for trying to kill them.

"Take us to my place," Luke demanded.
The driver looked at him through the rear view mirror.
"I must report this!" he cried.
"Do what you have to do, but after you take us to my home. I'll
call the authorities from there."
"But you're shot, sir. Maybe we should take you to a hospital and
have it looked at."

Luke shook his head in disagreement.
 "It's not that terrible. Just get me and my friend to the address I
gave you, right away."

Luke pressed a damp cloth against his sore neck as he thanked
the two Chicago detectives who had responded to their calls, and
showed them to the door. His phone rang urgently and Luke
motioned for Samiha to answer it as he shook hands with the
detectives and closed the door behind them.

"That was your friend Jess, from the university," Samiha
explained.

"He's on his way over right now." She led him over the living room couch and took the cloth from him and looked at his wound.

"Are you sure you won't have a doctor look at that?"
Luke shook his head.
"It's not that serious."
She cleaned it with peroxide, then dressed the area with a small bandage.

"Luke, what do you suppose happened back there? Who did this, and why would they want to harm us?"

Luke shrugged his shoulders.
"The police have no clues and no suspects, and they're inclined to believe that it was just a random drive by that wasn't particularly meant for us. But I doubt that very seriously. If our adversaries back there discovered that we'd given them the slip, and didn't like it, God only knows what they might have on their minds."

The phone rang again just then. This time Luke answered it.
"Please let him up," he directed to the party on the other end of the line.
"It's Jess," Luke announced.
"He's here. Get the door for him, will you?"

His friend Jess, and associate from the university, rushed to Luke's side as soon as Samiha let him in. He nodded a brief greeting to her, then took a seat next to his long time friend and looked with concern at the bandage on his neck.

"Jesus Luke!" he began.
"What the hell's going on?"
Luke smiled at him.
"You're not gonna believe what we've been through the past few days. I couldn't go into a lot of detail over the phone about what

Samiha's crew uncovered at the dig, but we were able to smuggle it out the country and we have it here now."
Jess rose and shook Samiha's hand.
"It's great to finally meet you," he told her.
"Luke's spoken so often and very highly of you."

She smiled at him. Jess turned back to his friend with a look of confusion.
"You can tell me all about it later, but in the meantime, this shooting... I'm absolutely stunned! Sure it's not uncommon here in the city, but to have it happen to someone close... I just can't believe it!"
"Jess, I have a feeling that the incident is related. I think we were shot at *because* of what she found."
"Really? Well, tell me about it. What exactly did you two find out there?"

Luke studied his friend's eyes for a moment before explaining.
"The reason for why I couldn't discuss the details on the phone is because we needed to be cautious, and we know without a doubt, that what her digger accidentally stumbled upon, is probably the most significant find ever unearthed in the history of archeology."
"Wow. Pretty tall words!" Jess exclaimed. Luke grinned at him, then rose from the couch and opened his leather overnight bag and removed the Ocular. Duct tape still attached the camcorder to the Ocular and Jess was puzzled as Luke set the entire thing into his lap.

"This part is conventional," Luke explained, indicating the camcorder.
"The other is much, much older."
"It looks like something you picked up at a garage sale," Jess remarked as he studied the contraption.

Luke went on,
"I attached the Ocular to the camcorder to be able to record everything we saw, but you can easily see the differences. The

Time Ocular as we've begun to call it, was built and left here by
extraterrestrials and is a receiver of some sort that allows one to
view whatever happened in the past at whatever given location
one happens to have it pointed in."
Jess contemplated his words for a few moments then said,
"Huh?"
"It sees into the past," Luke repeated.
 "You dial in any given moment by touching the bottom then it
automatically focuses into different times, from a few minutes
ago to thousands of years. So far, we're not even sure how far
back it can see, but we're positive that it looks back many
thousands of years."

Jess was dumbfounded, and became even more astonished as the
full meaning of Luke's explanation started to sink in.
"Really? It really does that?" he uttered in reverent awe.
Luke nodded.
"It really does. Come over here with me to the balcony. I'll show
you."

Luke took the machine from Jess's lap and walked over to the
sliding glass patio door and swung it open. From his sixteen-story
elevation the view overlooking Lincoln Park converged with the
banks of Lake Michigan . He raised the Ocular to eye level then
traced the bottom of it with the needle. It took several minutes or
scanning and adjusting before he was satisfied with what he had
found. For another moment he studied the scene, then a smile
began to form on his face that grew wider the longer he watched.
He chuckled as he held the needle in place and motioned for Jess
and Samiha to take a look.

"The first man to step on the territory known later as Chicago ,
was a black man!" he laughed, then continued,
 "I give you the team of Marquette and Joliet."

Samiha and Jess shared the viewfinder while Luke steadied it for
both of them to see. Luke had tuned into the banks of Lake
Michigan where the mouth of the Chicago River greeted it. Jess

gasped and Samiha giggled at the sight of several ancient canoes filled with men and equipment as they paddled to shore, hundreds of years before. The first of the team included the black man, a worker, and others who appeared to be in charge, as they waved the following canoes in.

"If you recall your history, Marquette and Joliet were turned back up the Mississippi River when warned of hostile Indians long before reaching their Gulf of Mexico destination. Instead, taking the advise of friendly natives, they came back up this way, along the Chicago River and finally here where they appear to be just landing.

"Of course this all occurred in the sixteen-seventies."

"Jesus!" exclaimed Jess as his eye remained glued to the sights below. He was profoundly astonished.

Luke lowered the Ocular and pulled away the needle, shutting the machine off, before handing it to Samiha, who returned it to its case.

Jess ran his hands through his hair while his eyes bugged with excitement.

"Holly shit!" he cried.

"Do you have any idea what this means? Holy shit!" he repeated.

"I know what it means," Luke acknowledged.

"I also suspect that others also know what it means, and don't want something like this to get out."

Jess continued to rave,

"Oh my God! You were right. This is as serious as anything could be. A discovery like this can literally change everything we know about anything in history!"

Luke quieted him with a raised hand and motioned for him to sit.

"Listen, Jess," Luke began.

"We just left a site near the Great Pyramid, where that single structure is comprised of over two and a half million carefully placed blocks of stone, none lighter than two-thousand pounds and most averaging over eighty-thousand pounds. The big ones, at the base, weigh nearly one hundred and sixty thousand pounds and at the time modern archeologists first began to study it, technology of the day might have been able to move a block of stone only fourteen thousand pounds.

"Some of the seams where the blocks meet cannot even be detected for precision that was used to set them together, and we haven't a clue as to how they were even able to cut anything that big.
"Finding this Time Ocular in that location, where we've been witnessing the remains of advanced technology for a lot of years now, just adds more credibility to the theories that something or someone other than the typical residents of the time, aided the locals, not only in the construction of the pyramids, but also in every day life.

"They accomplished things that even now, with all of our own technological skills, we still cannot duplicate."
Luke went on to explain to Jess how they had recorded the man who originally buried the Ocular, and showed him the stone carving of the planets, and relayed their unusual viewing of the Martian at his camp site.

"Unbelievable!" Jess remarked, when Luke had finished describing the events of the past few days.
"So what now? Where do you go from here?" he asked Luke.

"I'll tell you what now," Luke echoed.
"We're scientists and archeologists, teaches and students of the truths of what actually happened long ago. We now have in our possession the greatest tool that anyone in our profession could ever dream for. We can put away our pick axes and dust brushes for the time being and use something that can guarantee indisputable proof of the *real* truths, and preserve that tool with all of our might. We'll keep it out of the hands of people who would use it for their own selfish interests and use it with the proper application that would benefit everyone."

The phone rang again just then and Samiha rose to answer it. "Luke, this might be bigger than we can handle. I understand how critical this discovery is, but the implications...." He was interrupted when Samiha retuned, crying softly and holding her face in her hands.

"That was the attorney, Mr. Wienstien. Joseph is dead."

&

Chapter Sixteen

Two suited individuals announced themselves as FBI agents, when Jess led them into the residence.
"Luke Ozman called you," Jess explained.
"He's in the other room."

Jess motioned for them to follow him into the living area where Luke was still trying to console Samiha, who had not stopped crying over the loss of her dear friend.

"Hello Mister Ozman. My name is Judy and I'm with the FBI. This is my partner Michael." They displayed their ID and Luke offered them seats on a couch near them.

"Thanks for coming," Luke began.
"I hope I did the right thing by calling you and that maybe you can help us."
"We'll certainly do our best," she offered, then went on,
"We understand that you've been through a trying experience lately, both here and overseas, and we need your account on everything that happened. Do you believe that your shooting and the deaths of your co-workers, as you described to us over the phone, are related?"
"Very much so," Luke replied, and he continued,
"We think that is has to do with this." He showed her the stone carving of the planets.

"This was recovered from a site we were excavating near the Great Pyramid."
Judy accepted the carving from him and inspected it carefully.
"It's very old, huh?" she asked.
"Very!" Luke acknowledged.
"Why do you suppose anyone would want to harm you over this?" she asked, as her trained eyes studied his.

"We don't know. That's why we called you. We work for the University at Loyola and our duties take us and various other teams all over the world, on similar expeditions. Nothing like this has ever happened to us before."

Judy listened to him carefully as she looked around the apartment and noted the many awards and plaques that hung in frames on his walls.

"Our friend Joseph was killed," Samiha cried.
 "And another young boy barely in his teens, who worked as a digger for me."
Judy was very sympathetic. She moved closer to Samiha and knelt beside her, reaching out to hand to stroke her long dark hair in a comforting gesture.

"We're here to try and help. We realize that you've been through a lot lately, but I promise, I'll do everything in my power to keep you safe from here on out."
"We were able to speak to your taxi driver by phone just a few minutes ago," the other agent introduced as Michael offered.
"He confirmed every detail and right now we're running down every possible lead."
Judy directed her next question to Luke.

"Do you have any idea who may be responsible for this?"
"None," Luke answered while shaking his head.
 "I suspect that we may have ruffled the feathers of the local officials in charge of overseeing the activities of foreign excavators like us, but even that doesn't make much sense."

Judy pondered his words for a moment before responding.
"Are you quite sure that you're telling me everything you know?"
"Yes," he lied.
 "I have absolutely no idea why anyone would want to hurt us, except for the possibility that this carving may have some special significance."
"Ok," Judy uttered as she rose to her feet.

"Michael and I are going to keep a close eye on you for the next few days. We've been assigned to watch over you, and make sure that whomever is behind all of this be kept from harming you in the future.

"But I'd like to make one thing very clear. I make my living with my nose. And right now my nose tells me that you're not leveling one-hundred percent with me. I believe that you know a bit more than you're sharing with us. Just remember that we're on your side, and if there's something else you'd like to discuss with us, feel free to do so anytime."

Luke nodded in genuine appreciation.
"Thank you," he told her.
She handed him her business card.
"My cell phone number. Call me day or night. We won't be far away."

Luke smiled at them and thanked them again.
Jess agreed to stay the night after Luke refused to take no for an answer. Once Samiha had fallen asleep he called the attorney.

"I couldn't tell her everything on the phone," Weinstien explained, and he went on, "I learned that your man Joseph was tortured. They found his body dumped in a garbage bin some distance away from his home, in the rear fields. His two fore fingers had been severed at the knuckles by what was believed to have been caused by piano wire. They literally twisted off both of them, one by one, in a torture technique that I've seen before.

"They beat him too. Very badly for a long time, and then they shot him. From the looks of his body, they were with him quite some time before he died. It appears that he took a great deal of abuse, probably because he did not tell them what they wanted to know right away.

"But I can assure you, they did not leave empty handed. No one could've endured what he did, without cracking. I'm positive the killers did not leave before he told them whatever it was they wanted to know."

Luke clenched the receiver of the phone tightly as his anger mounted. Neither spoke for a few moments, then Weinstien broke the silence.

"What do you want me to do?" he asked.
"I want you to be careful," Luke replied, with urgency.
"But try to keep an eye on what's going on over there and let me know if there's anything you can find out about who might be responsible."
"I will," he acknowledged, then very solemnly he added,
"I'm very sorry for your loss mister Ozman. Joseph was such a nice man."

Luke hung up the phone.
Jess was awake and could see from the expression on Luke's face that something was very wrong.

"What was that about?" he asked.
Luke relayed what Weinstien reported.
"He described in detail of how Joseph was brutally tortured and murdered. It appears they forced him to tell everything he knew and how our welcome party came to greet us in the taxi last night."
Jess shook his head sadly. Luke went on.

"Tomorrow, very early, we're gonna see and record the ones who shot at us. I'll go back to the scene of the shooting, and using the Ocular, I'll get close enough to see every pore in their ugly faces and be able to establish a starting point for how to trace their movements back to find out where they came from and who they answer to."

Jess's eyes lit up with interest.
"The machine!" he exclaimed.
"It'll show it all to you!"
"Yes," Luke responded as he looked over at the leather case that contained the Ocular.
Jess added,
"That thing is gonna shake the world!"
"The world needs a little shaking," Luke muttered angrily.

"You see," the older one said to his younger companion,
 "Our earthly brethren have a history of evolution not different from our own, in that at some point, along their way, *Real Man* lost his way and began to look upon himself as a person separate and apart from *Source*, under what he considered to be a necessity to make a living, provide for his family, and later to protect himself and his community from neighboring people who had also lost the awareness of their true nature and their connection with *Source*.

"And in seeking out their livelihoods while struggling to survive, they cared not how they gained it. Whether earning or stealing or going to war, they justified their intentions with newly formed positionalities and grievances. Thus developed this current world of humans, each one of which looks upon himself as an individual separate and apart from all others, with his own interests and with a newly acquired 'responsibility' to provide for his current state of living and that of his future."

"This three-dimensional man, the man of earth, lives in a world circumscribed by his own limited concept of himself and his surroundings. Having no other point of reference than what the body's eyes can see, feel, touch, taste and smell, he is convinced that in order to survive he must lie, cheat, steal and go to war with others who he perceives as a threat.

"This is his life here now, ignorant of the truth that beyond his limited thinking, within the essence of his consciousness is another realm, much more glorious and all encompassing, with no need for force or might.

"Lost from his awareness, as liken to a dream state, he perceives all things to be outside and apart from himself, and he the victim of circumstances and events beyond his control. He believes he must attack or defend in order to stay alive."

 The younger companion nodded in agreement and he said, "They still exist in the stage of evolution unaware of who and where they really are."

Samiha's coffee filled the room with aromatic delight the next morning as she gently shook Luke and kissed him on the cheek. She set a cup of the steaming brew onto the table next to the couch where he'd slept and watched him as he rubbed the sleep from his eyes and sat up.

"What time is it?" he asked her.
"Early. Not yet six."
"Jess get up!" he shouted over to his friend who had curled up on another sofa across the room.

Jess mumbled something incoherent as if interrupted from a dream, then reluctantly opened his eyes and looked around to adjust his focus.

"Keep him from falling back asleep while I take a shower," Luke instructed Samiha.

"What are you going to do?" she asked him.

"I'm gonna return to the spot where the shots were fired at us, and using the Ocular, I'll focus in on the people who did it. I'll record it, bring it back here, and then we'll have a focal point from where to begin to trace exactly who these people are and where they came from."

"How long will you be gone?"

He shook his head.

"It shouldn't take more than an hour or so at the most. In the meantime I want you to take a stroll across the street and through the park for a few minutes, right before we leave. If our friends from the FBI are keeping tabs on us, as I suppose they are, they'll be watching you while Jess and I slip out the back way."

She nodded and smiled at him.

"Just don't be gone too long please. And be careful."

When Jess and Luke were both showered, dressed and ready, Samiha headed out for her walk. The two men watched from the balcony as she moved casually into the park amid a few dog walkers and joggers. They waited for a few minutes to give her a head start then left the apartment and took the service elevator down to the rear of the building.

They walked quickly together, Luke carrying the overnight case containing the Ocular and video recorder, ducking through the back alley and out on an adjacent side street. Jess flagged down the first taxi that passed and directed it to take them to the location near LaSalle street and Ontario , where the attack of the previous night took place.

When they arrived just a few minutes later, Jess asked the driver to wait.

"You don't mind do you? We just want to take a few quick pictures."

The cabbie nodded a silent reply while Luke and Jess exited the vehicle and looked around.

"It happened right here?" Jess asked.
"Right here." Luke echoed, as he pointed to an area directly across the street. There were still remnants of broken glass swept along the side of the curb, from the blown out taxi window. Luke removed the machine from its case and brought it up to eye level, then he retrieved the needle from his pocket and carefully ran it along the base of the Ocular until he was satisfied with the settings. Confidently, he began to scope the streets up one way, then the other, scanning the entire area in a sweeping motion for a few moments before he stopped moving and centered his attention on one spot. Jess could tell from the grim expression on Luke's face, that he'd dialed into the exact moment of the shooting.

"Here," Luke said as he handed the Ocular to his friend.
 "Take a look."
Jess's mouth dropped open slightly in amazement as he viewed the image of the event as it had occurred the night before. The cabbie watched them too, somewhat bewildered by their movements. Luke allowed Jess to look a little longer before taking the machine back. He then moved closer into the street and leaned slightly down, while he watched and recorded for another few minutes.

When he was finally satisfied, he lowered the Ocular and returned it to the overnight case.

"I have four faces on tape. The driver and the three others. Only two did the actual shooting. But now we have a place to start. We have the license plate number and perfect images of these guys. Later, when we resume the trace, we'll begin from here and back track to the airport and from O'Hare to their point of origin."

They got back into the taxi then and instructed the driver to drop them off a short distance from where they first hailed him. Back at the rear of his building Luke ushered Jess ahead of him as he hung back.

"You go first. Take the elevator, I'll use the stairs."
He waited until his friend was gone then entered the hallway that led to the rear stairwell. He managed to climb two or three steps before the sound of a familiar female voice stopped him in his tracks.

"What are you up to?" came the sudden and unexpected question from a dark corner behind the staircase. Luke was startled as he froze in his tracks. He looked back behind him and came face to face with Judy, the FBI agent.

"Did you think I'd fall for that goose chase? I've done this kind of thing a time or two before," she said, displaying a friendly smile.
Luke felt very stupid for a moment as he looked into her eyes.

"I don't know what I thought," he mumbled.
She moved closer to him with her arms folded disarmingly across her chest.

"Why don't you share with me a little. Tell me what's really going on here."

Luke sat down on the concrete steps and continued to gaze at her, still somewhat surprised by her abrupt appearance.
"I can't," he began.
"Not because I don't want to trust you, but I simply cannot tell you everything right now."
She studied his serious expression for a moment before responding.

"How am I supposed to help if you don't level with me? You called *us* remember?"
Luke nodded, silently contemplating an explanation. She continued.

"Getting shot in the middle of the afternoon in downtown Chicago , is not an every day occurrence. Someone is obviously very interested in you and it appears to me, that if they'd go to those extremes, I sincerely doubt they'd stop now. This isn't over by any means, and I want to know what it's really all about," she insisted.
Luke let out a sigh of discouragement. He hesitated before replying.

"I can't tell you right now. If I did, you'd have to file reports and inform your superiors. Then more reports would be documented and more people would know, and they'd have to tell others and before you knew it, everybody from here to China would know and that's exactly what I must avoid at all costs.

"I simply cannot take a chance that the wrong people find out something that is too critical to let out at this time. I'm asking you to bear with me, just for a little while. When the time is right, I'll tell you."
"That serious, huh?" she asked.
"Very!"

Her gaze moved from his face to the overnight bag he carried strapped to his shoulder.

"What's in there?"
Luke thought for a moment, then lowered the case and unzipped it, opening it and showing the contents.
"Video stuff?"
Luke just nodded.

She started to ask him why he was carrying around camera equipment and sneaking around through back alleys early in the morning, but decided against it and instead motioned for him to go on his way.

"Go on," she told him. "Get outta here. We'll talk again. But if you decide to change your mind about confiding in me, you have my number."

Luke closed the case back up and rose to his feet.
"Thanks for understanding."

"She's very intelligent," Luke remarked to Samiha and Jess once he was back upstairs in the apartment.
"What did she want?" Samiha asked apprehensively.
"She suspects something is up," Luke explained.
"She knew all along that we weren't telling her everything, but she didn't press me. She's concerned and very understanding, but I have a feeling that she's also very persistent, someone who'll want to dig a little deeper."

"So what now, Luke?" Jess asked him.
"Well, I don't know if calling the FBI was such a great idea now. Having them over our shoulders every minute of the day will restrict our movements and prevent us from doing the kind of investigation we need to accomplish very quickly.

"We need some other place to work from... somewhere that isn't monitored by our new FBI friends, and uncompromised with the probability that the shooters themselves may find us here. It's just a matter of time before they get my address."
Luke thought about the problem for a moment then suddenly remembered something that perked his attention.

"Wait a minute! What about Leo? He'd help us!"
Jess nodded in agreement. Leo was another professor at the University who lived on the north shore of Lake Michigan in a very affluent neighborhood where five thousands square foot

houses were considered average sized. He taught astronomy and even built his own private observatory in an elaborate and very expensive addition on his property.

"Leo wouldn't think twice about helping out," Jess remarked, and he went on, "We could certainly trust him, and I bet that he'd be thrilled to see the stone carving of the planets."
"Well, let's go see him," Luke suggested, and then added,
 "But this time, we'll be a little more discreet about how we leave so as to minimize our chances of being seen."
"How are we going to do that?" Samiha asked him.
"I have an idea," Luke said. "Jess, first give Leo a call and make sure he's at home."

Less than an hour later the three of them huddled in the rear hallway of Luke's building. Jess carried an extra overnight bag filled with a few important personal items, and Samiha took along the light luggage she'd brought with for the trip. Luke peered anxiously in anticipation down the alley his residence, and very soon saw the unmistakable image of a large white pizza delivery van as it lumbered toward them.

The driver, a young man barely past his teens, pulled the truck very close to the back doorway and jumped out. He opened a sliding door on the side of his vehicle, then entered the building where Luke greeted him warmly.

"Johnny, you're a lifesaver," Luke praised him, as he smiled widely. The young man grinned at the three of them, then motioned for all to get aboard.

"One of my favorite students," Luke explained to Samiha as they pulled away from the building.

"How did you explain to him why we needed to be picked up like this?" Samiha asked him.
"I didn't. I just offered him $50 for a ride."

Chapter Seventeen

Leo's house was located in the quaint near north suburb of
Wilmette . When his parents passed away, they left him this
sprawling gated estate built on enough land to easily
accommodate two more homes of equal size. Leo had improved
the property with a massive two story addition that was topped
off with a giant glass dome that served as his window to the
heavens, and accommodated one of the largest privately owned
telescopes ever built and installed on residential property.

Luke and Jess greeted their friend Leo with warm hugs and
handshakes.
"This is Samiha, from the Giza project."
Leo was very large man, easily four hundred pounds and very
tall. His demeanor was always jovial and wide smile ever present
and delightfully gracious.

"So happy to meet you," he said as he took her hand and kissed it
gently.
"Please, all of you, follow me," he invited.
He led them through a spacious entry area, then through the short
hall that opened up into his observatory addition.

"This is where I spend most of my time," he explained as he
waved an arm around the massive room. Jess took Samiha's
luggage and set down next to the wall, while Luke gazed around
in awe.
"What a lab!" he exclaimed. "This is absolutely wonderful," he
added.

The entire roof was the glass observation dome, and built directly
into an overhead swiveling concavment was the telescope, that
protruded out easily fifteen feet and ended at a control desk area
set up on circular platform that raised the high backed seating
some six inches off the floor. Surrounding the base was a neatly

constructed custom-made counter area and work-place, that accommodated his computers, keyboards, and file cabinets.

"That's fairly new," Leo explained as he pointed to one wall and the biggest flat screen television monitor any of them had ever seen.
"Jeeze!" Samiha exclaimed.
"I didn't realize they made one that large!"
"I had it specially designed and constructed," Leo explained.
"It's like your own Omni Max!" Jess added with a grin.
"That's the idea," Leo explained as he let out a loud reverberating chuckle. "It allows me to transfer images from the telescope to the screen and blow up details hundreds of times their actual size."

Around the observation platform were several large sofas, and Leo motioned for all of them to sit while he settled into his favorite chair near his desk.
"Jess's brief phone call was very interesting, to say the least," he began. "So tell me, how can I help?"

Luke smiled at him.
"First, I want to thank you for letting us into your home. I think you'll agree that what I'll share with you now might shock a lot of people, but we're all scientists here, and not strangers to things out of the ordinary.

"One of Samiha's crew discovered something very remarkable a few days ago, and since then, there has not been a single dull moment."

Leo listened with growing attention as Luke recounted the events of the recent few days, describing the Ocular, how it worked, the person who originally buried it, and all of the circumstances leading up to their meeting with the two Feds. Luke left nothing out and when he was finished he could tell that Leo was totally mesmerized.

The large man suddenly stood up from his chair and moved quickly over to one of his file cabinets. He fumbled through several files for a few anxious minutes before he finally found what he was looking for. He removed an old manila folder and leafed through it before handing it to Luke.

"Take a look at those photographs and read the captions," he instructed.
"Does your machine look like that one?" Luke's immediate reaction was astonishment as he stared at pictures of an exact duplicate of the Ocular.

"Where did you get these?" he almost shouted.
"Some buried government archives via the Freedom of Information Act. At the time, I was looking for some information relating to the Mariner flight NASA conducted when it sent the probe to Mars in the mid seventies, on its mission to map the surface. Quite by accident, I stumbled upon these. Most of the pages had been blotted out and censored, but enough remained to make the find interesting."

Luke passed the pages to Samiha. On one of them was a full page photo of the Ocular, and under it, the caption, *Sodmein Cave Discovery*.
Luke picked up the leather shoulder case and unzipped it. He removed the Ocular and held it out for Leo to inspect.

"Oh my Lord!" Leo exclaimed, as he reverently accepted the machine into his large hands, and turned it over and over, while his eyes grew wide with excitement.

"The video cam I taped to it is an extension that allows me to record what the Ocular sees," Luke explained.

"Good idea," Leo remarked.
"I was just thinking," Luke went on, "that we could probably attach it to your telescope somehow, and maybe even see the collision of whatever it was that struck Jupiter and caused the

birth of Venus, and helped to destroy some of the surface on Mars."

Leo was already a step ahead of him. He moved over to his desk top and carefully took away the duct tape from Luke's makeshift connection, then searched his cabinets for clamps that he could use to attach the Ocular to the viewfinder of his telescope. He moved like an eager child with bowl of ice cream.

He darted from drawer to cabinet as his three guests looked on while he furiously prepared the things he would need to get started. After a few minutes he turned back to Luke.

"From what you've shared with me on how you've operated the Ocular, I'm going to have to make a few adjustments because looking out into space with your machine and searching for a particular time associated with an object, is a bit more complex than viewing it directly here on Earth. To find Jupiter, I'll have to calibrate exactly where the planet *was* not *is*, do you understand?"

"Makes sense to me," Luke replied.

"So," Leo continued,

"I'll need to attach the Ocular to the telescope, then backward trace the revolutions of both Mars and Jupiter, until I achieve the desired time line, when the event actually occurred."

Jess and Luke both nodded in agreement.

"So how long before you're able to do that?" Samiha asked him.

"Not long," he replied.

"Give me a few minutes."

Leo set to the task of mounting the Ocular to his telescope, then started his computations.

"Give me that needle thing," he asked Luke, and went on.

"I won't need your duct tape or this video cam any more," he joked.

Luke handed him the Ocular's needle and they all watched as the big man focused his concentration on peering through the Ocular while he touched a few buttons on his keyboard. Slowly, and

with a quiet hum, the overhead swivel moved ever so slightly, until it stopped at the position Leo wanted. He carefully turned a large dial on the right side of the telescope, while holding the needle under the base of the Ocular with his other hand.
He remained motionless for several minutes until finally, his expression began to take on a look of utter amazement. His mouth dropped open as he pressed his eyes against the twin protrusions of the Ocular's viewfinder and gripped the side of the telescope with a new urgency.

"Oh my God!" he suddenly exclaimed.
"What is it?" Luke demanded.
Leo's face was pale with disbelief when he uttered,
 "Your friend from Mars wasn't kidding! This is the most spectacular thing I have ever seen!"

Leo flipped a switch on his control board and instantly the big screen on the wall came to life in an explosion of color and light, and a clear image of two planets.
 "That's Jupiter," Leo said as he pointed to the larger of the two celestial bodies, which loomed in the background, easily 15 times bigger than Mars.

"The smaller one is Mars and the two appear to be almost in direct alignment. Now watch the upper left corner of the screen. The next thing you'll see will be the comet that emerges from the other side of Jupiter."

Seconds later the comet appeared, streaking into the horizon of Jupiter's massive aura, and swinging around into a captured orbit with neck breaking velocity.

"Damn!" Jess muttered.
 "That sucker is huge!"
"The biggest comet I ever saw!" Samiha acknowledged. All eyes remained glued to the screen as the comet suddenly broke into three separate pieces, and slammed almost simultaneously into Jupiter's surface. For several moments, the screen became

blurred with a sudden flash of red, then it refocused to display the images of the unmerciful havoc that had just been created.

The comet hit Jupiter so violently, that a large chunk of the planet's crust was literally ripped away, and was now spinning uncontrollably out to space in the direction of Mars. Smaller pieces of the newly formed chunk fought to stay together, as fire and explosions ravaged its surface.

Soon all signs of the giant comet dissipated, leaving only a gaping red spot on Jupiter's body, and the new born planet raced forward, gaining momentum with every passing second.

"Alas!" Leo cried.
" I give you The Great Red Spot of Jupiter and the birth of Venus!"
The new planet streaked to the foreground and headed straight for Mars.

"Now pay attention." Leo shouted.
"Watch what happens when she passes Mars!"

They all watched with growing anticipation as the brand new fireball sped past the slightly smaller red planet and began to spew debris in its wake. Mars was suddenly bombarded with a devastating flurry of rock that all struck one side of the planet. Each seemed to fight one another in a spectacular display of exchange, until a few minutes passed and Venus proceeded on its new course in orbit around the Sun.

"Whew!" Luke exclaimed.
"That was astonishing!" And he went on,
"Now we know how the asteroid belt was formed, and why Mars's two moons look so strangely out of proportion."
"Venus is on fire still, to this very day!" Leo commented.
"It's surface is a constant upheaval of volcanic activity, and now we know why and how it all came about."

He turned to Luke and Samiha and added.
"You have one hell of a machine here! Of course you'll stay here with me and together we'll come up with a solution for these characters who are trying to take it away from you."

Luke acknowledged his offer with a friendly nod.
"Great. Thank you. I still don't feel very comfortable with the idea of putting friends in jeopardy but if there were any other way..."
Leo dismissed his apology with a wave of his hand.

"Never mind," he assured Luke.
"This discovery is much too significant. "Tell me what you've managed to learn so far."
"We already have some good close-ups of the shooters." Luke went on.
"That's a start. Now all I need is to pinpoint exactly who is responsible... who the people are who are so determined in their efforts to separate us from the ocular."

Leo nodded, while carefully pondering his next words.
"We have to assume that these people, whomever they are, really mean business and will stop at nothing until they get what they want."
Luke agreed.
"You're right of course."
Leo smiled at them.
"So it's settled. You'll be my guests here for as long as you like. Now, how do you plan to trace the movements of these shooters?"
"Wherever they came from, they left a permanent visual record, easily traced with the machine. I'm gambling that once we know who they are we may learn other things about them that they might not want made public. With the right information on them we may be in a better place to bargain.

"We also have to assume that they know everything there is to know about our discovery... maybe even be in the possession of

the one from the Sodmein Cave find. If they don't, I'd be surprised. Assuming all of this, we're gonna have to be particularly careful about how we accomplish all of this."
"Well," Leo interrupted, "I happen to have the perfect vehicle to help with getting around and following their movements without drawing a lot of attention. You'll need it for the kind of snooping you'll be doing. "It's a conversion van."

Leo referred to his customized RV Conversion, a typical recreational van converted with high backed swivel chairs, a table near the rear and screened windows with blinds.

"It's perfect for what you have in mind. You can sit in the back with the Ocular while one of us drives. It'll provide you with all the cover you need to zoom in on your subjects while you trace their movements."
"Sounds great," Luke acknowledged. "Let's have a look at it."

After submitting their required FBI activity reports, Judy and Michael were unexpectedly summoned to their supervisor's office. Such meetings were not uncommon but still rare enough to arouse more than a little concern.

Chapter Eighteen

The Special Agent in charge ushered them into his office and motioned for them to sit.
"Something crossed my desk last night that you two need to be aware of." His tone was very serious and urgent. He handed them each a manila file folder then continued as they listened intently. "This morning my bosses brought to my attention the fact that we've been observing the activities of an Israeli group of mercenary spies lately and have reason to believe that they are responsible for the attack on your two new archeologist friends.

"Mercenary spies?" Judy echoed.
Her boss nodded then went on.
"Paid professionals," he explained. "Sub-contractors for lack of a better term. The government over there uses them in special instances whenever it wouldn't be diplomatically safe to commission their own agencies.

"All of them are ex-military from one branch of the service or another and all seasoned pros in their own fields related to surveillance and other expertise."

Michael interrupted him.
"So these guys are used to do the dirtiest work... kind of like unofficial ventures that require no accounting for their actions?"
"Exactly right. What's more, they all enjoy congressional immunity as a result of mutual agreements between our government and theirs that were established years ago when circumstances made it necessary for us to employ the same types."
"So what are they up to?" Judy asked, her expression very concerned.
Her boss motioned for them to open the file folders.
"They appear to be very interested in whatever it was that your friends found buried and dug up."

"We saw what they found," Judy offered.

"It was a very old flat rock with some kind of carved drawing inscription."

"That's not all they found," he continued.

"Turn to the third page, to the three photos."

He waited until they had done as instructed and watched their reactions before going on.

The photo page was captioned *Sodmein Cave Discovery* and depicted three views of something that looked like a very large video camcorder with strange double ocular eye protrusions for viewing. The explanatory text below the pictures described the object as something that had been discovered after having been buried thousands of years before.

"Before I continue any further I need you two to pay special attention to what I am about to tell you. I've been instructed to inform you that this is to be regarded with the utmost secrecy. "Don't talk about it with anyone."

As Judy examined the photo page and read the information her eyes widened with increased nervous interest.

"I saw this thing," she announced.

"I saw this thing in Luke Ozman's bag when I stopped him in his rear stairway the other day! I thought it was video equipment of some kind!"

Her boss appeared to become even more concerned. He rubbed his chin nervously then continued.

"What you saw was a machine that looks just like it. That one, we've known for quite a while now, has been in the possession of the Israelis for years. And here's the best part. From what we've been able to gather about that thing is that it has some remarkable capabilities. Sources tell us that this machine, though thousands and thousands of years old, is a mechanical device so sophisticated that it can actually look into the past and see what went on wherever it points, to whatever time is chosen."

Judy and Michael just stared at their boss in dumbfounded awe
for what seemed a long time before Michael broke the silence.
"Help me understand. You mean that a machine can really do
Judy interrupted him.
"How can that be possible?" she almost screamed.
Her boss shook his head.

"I don't know all of the science details, but I've been assured
that it works on very believable principals of high resolution
optics. Some intelligence built those things a long time ago and
left them here. Who or why we can only guess, but there's no
disputing the fact that they work.

"The biggest problem about all this is it's already starting to
escalate into something very unmanageable. We don't need that
nonsense. We need that machine."

He took the file folders from out of their hands then moved back
behind his desk and sat in his chair.
"We need that machine," he repeated.
"Once it's in our possession and everyone concerned knows it,
we eliminate the need for this group of thugs to run around here
shooting at people and disturbing the peace."
"You want us to get it?" Michael asked.
His boss didn't answer his question. Instead he tucked the file
folders into one of his desk drawers, then looked at them both
intently before speaking.

"I want you to think about everything we've discussed. Think of
the possibilities. Just imagine what can be learned with a tool of
the capabilities that machine has. Think about the disruption it
could cause to the very foundation of our society and its values,
traditions, and laws if it revealed something the public just isn't
ready for yet.
"Then I want you to stick to this like white on rice. I want
constant updates. I want to know about every single person who
comes in contact with this machine and your two friends. Before

we can just go in and confiscate something of this magnitude from influential scientists we need to know everything, and soon. "And I need you to keep this all between us three. The fewer people that know the better. Now get going."

"There's one more big advantage we have," Leo explained to Luke as he led Jess and him into his massive six-car garage where the conversion van was kept.
"What's that?"
"The big screen I have isn't just another one of my toys. From time to time, whenever called on, I entertain corporate meetings run by a real estate developer who just happens to own his own satellite, completely armed with high-visual zoom technology and photographic relay equipment. The damn thing can read news print from a hundred and fifty mile high orbit."
"You're kidding."
"Nope! A couple times a month this guy brings over a team of people to view real estate property locations for future development sites. They all sit around as I zoom in on a given area and transfer it onto the big screen."
"Some toy," Jess offered.

Leo bellowed out a laugh. "The thought just occurred to me that I could probably hook up your time ocular to it, and maybe even be able to conduct a few snoop sessions right from here!"
"Well, that's brilliant!" Luke exclaimed.
"Do you think you can?"
"I don't see why not. If you could do it with an outdated video cam and some duct tape, I think I might be able to scrounge up some improvising equipment of my own. I probably won't use duct tape though," he added with another healthy laugh.

Luke's mental wheels were churning at full speed.
"Can you just imagine what we could accomplish... what we could see? Wow!"
"There's no limit to the possibilities," Leo agreed, with a wide smile.

"Well, OK then," Luke announced. "We've seen the van, and yes, it's perfect for doing some local scouting missions. But for now, why don't you show me what that satellite can do."
Leo led them back into his screen room and Luke took a seat next to Samiha who had begun to doze off on a couch.
"What's going on?" she asked him.
Luke said nothing as he watched Leo begin to make a few settings on a computer at his desk, then move to the center of the room to where he pointed to the eyepiece of the massive telescope that loomed high over-head and protruded through the glass dome roof.

"What I had in mind," Leo began,
"was to bounce the image trajectory right off the satellite's telescopic mirror. In other words, while the satellite is looking at something down here, we could be looking at what it's looking at. Understand?"
Luke nodded. "Go on."
Leo continued.
"The magnifying strength of my telescope will enhance the range of the ocular, just like it did when we looked at the images of the Mars disaster. Only instead of looking out into space, we'll be reversing the image and be able to see anything the satellite points at down here."
"That makes sense," Jess offered.
Leo continued.
"First let me show you what this satellite can do." Looking at his watch he went on.
"Right now the satellite should be about thirty-five degrees north longitude and one-hundred-ten west latitude, which should place it right above the Rocky Mountain range over the Arizona/Nevada area. Watch the screen. I'll tune it in right now."

They all observed with great interest as the giant screen lit up with a sudden blur of color and indistinguishable features. Leo adjusted the focus by typing a few quick codes on the keyboard of his computer, while he watched the screen. Very soon a clear picture of landscape appeared as seen from one hundred and fifty miles above the earth.

"OK. I'm gonna zoom in closer now."
With a few more clicks of the keyboard the images on the screen began to grow larger and larger as the mountains became more clear and defined. Leo turned his chair to face the screen and kept a finger on one of the keys. Every time he pressed it, the image appeared to become closer and closer until it seemed as if the view had loomed to only a few hundred feet off the ground.
"OK. Now we're looking at an area of desert with nothing much interesting going on, but watch when I do this."

He pressed the up arrow on his keyboard and instantly the scene moved to widen the view to the north, and include a larger view of the terrain.
"I moved the lens on the satellite's camera ever so slightly just then."
"Amazing!" Jess exclaimed.
"Pretty neat huh?" Leo boasted.
"Now comes the interesting part." He rose from his chair and picked up the ocular, then as before, he strapped it securely to the end of telescope and began making a few calibrations back at his computer.
"Right now, I'm lining up the visual sighting between the telescope and the very center of telescopic mirror on the satellite. Once I pinpoint it, I'll lock it in to synchronize with the movement of the satellite, so that as that big tin can up there moves in orbit, my telescope will move with it and keep everything we're looking at in view."

Luke gave Samiha a wink and shrugged his shoulders, smiling.
"You're the doctor."
Leo seemed to be talking more to himself as he went on.
"As soon as it's perfectly aligned we should be able to use the Ocular."
He continued to make a few more adjustments, both at the computer and back at the end of the telescope. After a few

minutes he stepped back to look at the Ocular then breathed out a long sign of anticipation.

"Well, here goes. Let's hope this thing works."
He touched the base of the Time Ocular with the ancient needle and the now-familiar low hum of the machine coming to life filled the silence of the room.

"Watch the screen. This should be interesting," Leo directed as he slowly moved the needle along the smooth bottom of the Ocular. At once the image on the massive screen began to change.
"It's working!" Samiha exclaimed excitedly.
They all watched the screen with renewed interest as the desert terrain, very gradually began to show shifts in color, shape and ground features. Green plant life loomed into view where only seconds before only barren rocks and sandy soil existed. In just a few seconds they had witnessed thousands of years of evolutionary transformation.

Cactus stumps were now replaced with trees, surrounded by tall grass and wild flowers. Lush shrubbery, lagoons filled with water and strange plant life teamed everywhere. Leo stopped moving the needle for a moment and paused to allow everyone to enjoy the new view.

Small animals scurried along the ground and colorful birds of varying sizes dotted the trees while in the northern distance they could see a river flowing with energetic activity.
All of them stared in awe for some time, suspended in reverent appreciation.
"This thing works better than I thought it would," Leo whispered.
"It's totally amazing!"
"It's like we're sitting on a balcony overlooking the back yard," Jess mumbled.
"Truly incredible!" Luke remarked.
"Can you pan the area a bit?"

Leo nodded and clicked on the right arrow button on the keypad. Immediately the view shifted to display more of the area to the right. Then he clicked the left arrow button and screen opened up more of the terrain in the opposite direction.

"I wonder how far back we went?" Samiha asked.

"Good question," Leo said.

"That'll be my next project... figuring out how to calibrate exactly where, or should I say, *when* we're looking at."

"We can save those projects for another time," Luke proclaimed. "For now, we have all of the calibration we need to find out who shot me and why they're so determined to keep this fantastic knowledge out of our hands."

෩

Chapter Nineteen

The elder of the two companions was speaking.
"Our brethren here will eventually come to the understanding that
they are not form. They are consciousness itself. They will fight
and they will defend and they will continue to distract themselves
with their own foggy perception of what they deem to be
'reality' until such a time comes to pass when they become weary
of their consistent failures.

"They are deeply rooted in what they perceive as Suffering. And
suffering is an emphasis upon all that the world has done
to injure him. Here is their world's demented version of
salvation clearly shown. Like to a dream of punishment, in
which the dreamer is unconscious of what brought on the
attack against himself, he sees himself attacked unjustly,
and by something not himself. He is the victim of this
"something else," a thing outside himself for which he has
no reason to be held responsible. He must be innocent
because he knows not what he does, but what is done *to*
him. Yet is his own attack upon himself apparent still, for it
is he who bears the suffering. And he can *not* escape
because its source is seen outside himself.

"Now you are being shown you *can* escape. All that is
needed is you look upon the problem as *it is*, and not the
way that you have set it up. How could there be another
way to solve a problem which is very simple, but has been
obscured by heavy clouds of complication, which were
made to keep the problem unresolved? Without the clouds,
the problem will emerge in all its primitive simplicity. The
choice will *not* be difficult, because the problem is absurd
when clearly seen. No-one has difficulty making up his
mind to let a simple problem be resolved, if it is *seen* as
hurting him, and also very easily removed.

"The "reasoning" by which the world is made, on which it rests, by which it is maintained, is simply this:
"YOU are the cause of what I do. Your presence *justifies* my wrath, and you exist and think *apart* from me. While YOU attack, I MUST be innocent. And what I suffer from *is* your attack." No-one who looks upon this "reasoning" *exactly* as it is could fail to see it does *not* follow, and it makes no sense. Yet it *seems* sensible because it *looks* as if the world *were* hurting you. And so it seems as if there is no *need* to go beyond the obvious in terms of cause.

"There is indeed a need. The world's escape from condemnation is a need which those *within* the world are joined in sharing. Yet they do not recognize their common need. For each one thinks that, if he does his part, the condemnation of the world will rest on him. And it is this that he perceives to be his part in its deliverance. Vengeance must have a focus. Otherwise, is the avenger's knife in his own hand, and pointed to himself. And he must see it in another hand, if he would be a victim of attack he did not choose. And thus he suffers from the wounds a knife he does not hold has made upon himself.

"This is the *purpose* of the world he sees. And, looked at thus, the world provides the means by which this purpose seems to be fulfilled. The means attest the purpose, but are not themselves a cause. Nor will the cause be changed by seeing it apart from its effects. The cause produces the effects, which then bear witness to the cause, and not themselves. Look, then, *beyond* effects. It is not here the cause of suffering and sin must lie. And dwell not on the suffering and sin, for they are but *reflections* of their cause. The part you play in salvaging the world from condemnation is your own escape.

"Forget not that the witness to the world of evil cannot speak except for what has seen a need for evil in the world. And this is where your guilt was first beheld. In separation from your brother was the first attack upon yourself begun.

And it is this the world bears witness to. Seek not another cause, nor look among the mighty legions of its witnesses for its undoing. They *support* its claim on your allegiance. What conceals the truth is not where you should look to find the truth. The witnesses to missing the mark all stand within *one* little space. And it is *here* you find the cause of your perspective on the world."

His younger companion silently contemplated every thought. There was a long silence between them as the night lingered on.

స్

Judy and Michael took up position, parked on the street very near to the front of the entrance of Luke's apartment building and settled in to prepare for a lengthy surveillance vigil. It was dark now, and they'd already spent several hours watching the movements of passers by and discretely scanning the occupants of cars that passed them in the street.

Judy used a small but very powerful pair of binoculars that worked effectively to help bring the entire area into clear view. She was engrossed as she examined a particular car that she had seen circle the block several times before in just the past few minutes. She handed the binoculars to her partner.

"Look over there," she directed as she pointed in the direction of the car she'd been scrutinizing.
 "There's fours guys in that vehicle, and I'm positive they're up to something. This is the third time I've seen them pass, moving really slowly."
"Yeah," Michael acknowledged.
 "I noticed that too."
Judy continued,

"Well, it might not be significant, but just in case, I'm gonna take a little stroll down the block."

The vehicle they saw had already turned left at the first corner as Judy switched on her portable radio, attached to her waist band and inserted an ear plug receiver into her left ear and under her hair.
Michael did the same.
"I'm set, go ahead," he told her.

She left the car and began walking nonchalantly down the street, past Luke's building and toward the corner where their suspicious car had just turned.
"Can you read me?" she asked as she spoke into a invisible button microphone attached to her collar.
"You're one hundred percent.... reading you clear," Michael responded.
"OK. Keep an eye on your rear. Watch for them to come back around the block." Judy stopped just before the corner and sat on a bench provided for CTA transit users while waiting for a local bus. Only a few minutes went by before Michael's voice crackled in her ear.

"Here they come again. It looks like they're gonna park."
This time the car pulled over to the curb directly in front of the building and stopped. Four men exited the vehicle and without hesitation, quickly entered through the front door.

"I'm going in," Judy announced.
"Wait three minutes then follow me." Judy got up from the bench and started to cross the street, when unexpectedly, her cell phone began to ring from inside her jacket's upper pocket. Once she got to the other side of the street she stopped at the curb and removed her phone.

"This is Judy." The voice at the other end of the line took her completely by surprise.
"Judy, this is Luke. Do not go into the building."

"Luke... Ozman?" she gasped.

"Yes. You gave me your cell phone number, remember?"

"Well, yeah, but..." Her voice trailed off as she displayed an expression of total disbelief."

"I can't explain right now," Luke continued.

"Just, please, do not go into my building after those guys. They're the ones who shot at me."

Judy was utterly confused and bewildered as her mind raced in a search for a logical explanation. Then everything she recalled about the meeting with her boss, earlier that day, came flooding back.

"OK. I'm going back to my car. You just stay on the line with me."

Michael jerked up in alarm and stared quizzically at her as she walked back to the car and slammed the door behind her.

"What's going on?" he demanded.

Judy raised her forefinger up to her lips to silence him as she continued to speak with Luke and leaned closer to Michael to allow him to hear.

"You and I have a lot to discuss," she said.

"For starters, could you kindly let me in on just how you know we're out here watching your place? Are you perched in a tree somewhere?"

"I can't go into a lot of detail right now Judy, for the reasons I explained to you before. You'll have to trust me a little while longer."

"No!" Judy shouted into the phone.

"It's about time you leveled with me. We know what you have in your possession... what you and your friends dug up, and we also know how critical this situation is becoming. This is all getting too sticky for your own good and everyone else involved. We need to sit down together and sort this all out before it gets completely out of hand."

"You know what I have in my possession?" Luke echoed.

"Yes. We've been briefed on your machine and what it can do."
Luke was silent for a moment before he went on.
"Well, if you know about it, then you're probably not totally in
the dark about the people who want to take it away from me."

Judy didn't answer and Luke continued.
 "Well now we will too. We've been tracing their origin all day.
We'll find out who they are, why they're here and even more. We
have reason to believe that they have an identical machine in
their own possession, a machine they've been using for their own
selfish interests for quite a while now."
"Listen Judy," Luke went on,
"I have a very good feeling about you. I believe that you are a
good person with good intentions, but right now I am forced to
not trust anyone. You're absolutely correct! This situation is very
critical, and the only way I know how to manage it is to keep out
of sight from everyone, including you, and remain that way until
we can eliminate any threat to us."
"And just how do propose to accomplish that?" Judy asked him.
"By turning the tables on the forces that are trying to prevent us
from using the machine," Luke answered. "It's very obvious to
me now that the selfish interests they've been pursuing probably
involve a lot of gathered information on things the US
government would rather the public not be informed of.
Damaging things. Things that would literally bring the roof down
upon every fiber of our institutions."
"Luke, I understand how you feel," Judy began.
 "I have good feelings about you too. But if you're right about
these damaging things, what possible good can come from
exposing information that would hurt people or create unrest?"
"It's not my intention to expose anything," he retorted.
"I just want to make sure that *they know that I know,* and that fire
can be fought with fire.
"I can't let you know where I am and I prefer that you not search
for me too diligently. But I promise to stay in touch with you and
keep you up to date on any new developments, so long as I can
continue do what I have to do."
"I can't promise anything, Luke," she told him,

"But I'll tell you what I'm gonna do right now. When those guys come out of your building we'll be there to greet them."
"Just be careful," Luke urged. "I'll call you back soon."
The phone went dead then and Judy returned it to her jacket pocket.
"Get your badge out and let's go," Judy blurted.
"Let's introduce ourselves to these guys."

Luke and his friends had stayed mesmerized in front of the large video screen while Leo worked all day at zoning in on various locations and times. At one point Leo had suggested that it be wiser to conduct their surveillance from the safety of his home whenever possible, and he proved it with successful and precise results. In only one afternoon they had comprised three full tapes of recorded documentation related to the men who had attacked Luke and Samiha in the taxi.

For now, the recorder and ocular were focused as they continued to watch the pair of FBI agents on the screen, via their eye in the sky satellite.

"There they are!" Jess announced as the four men who had recently disappeared into the building, emerged from the front entrance and walked right into the waiting presences of Judy and Michael. Judy approached them all with her identification held high in the air for all to see. The four men just stopped and appeared to be listening to her attentively.
Her expression wasn't very visible from the current angle but from her body language and the method in which she pointed her finger in their faces, it was apparent that her demeanor was anything but hospitable.

Luke smiled.
"She's letting them know in very clear terms that they don't run anything here in this country. I wish I were there!"
After several minutes of heated conversation the four men got back in their vehicle and sped away. Judy and Michael stayed for another few minutes before heading back to their own car. Before

entering the passenger's side Judy looked up at the night sky for a moment, then winked at nothing in particular.

"I wonder what she's thinking," Samiha muttered.

Luke smiled.

"If I were in her shoes right now I'd probably be pretty insecure about my own privacy."

Luke rose from his seat.

"Listen. It's late. Why don't you all get some rest. We'll have plenty to do in the morning."

"It's still early for me," Leo attested,

"but I'll show Jess and Samiha to a couple of guest rooms upstairs."

"What about you Luke?" Samiha asked him.

"I want to go over the tapes we recorded today when we traced those guy's movements. We need some still photographs of them following us and shooting at me. I have a plan that may help get them off our backs for good. I won't be long."

Samiha kissed him on the cheek and bid him goodnight before Leo led her and Jess out of the room. Luke selected the first of the tapes they'd comprised, loaded it into Leo's sophisticated video system then settled on a couch with the remote. When Leo returned, he joined him.

"Leo, who do we know in the news media. Does the University have a particular group of contacts that they rely on?"

Leo thought about his question for a few moments then shook his head.

"As far I know, we're not on a first name basis with any of the really heavy news anchors, if that's what you're referring to. But, we do use Steve Selser, the science editor at WTTW pretty regularly."

"That's the educational channel, right?"

Leo nodded.

"Yes. He calls on Jess and I all of the time looking for news-worthy opinions related to new or important science developments of one kind or another."

"Well then, he's perfect. That channel has a fairly large audience and lots of integrity. Without divulging *everything* about the Ocular we can still provide him with a story that will get a lot of attention and draw the kind of interest we need. We can give him photographs of the stone carving, the guys following us from the airport, the shooting, and their little chat with the FBI in front of my building, among other things."

"Not a bad idea," Leo confirmed.

"It would arouse some public interest and give you some bargaining power. And, I think that Steve would probably welcome any opportunity that would increase his own ratings."

"OK then. Let's put together a little package for him. We'll scan these tapes and create a pictorial scrap book on what we have so far."

Leo got up from his seat and searched his desk drawer until he found a pack of photo paper, then inserted it into the carriage of his printer. Luke turned on the video machine from the remote control, then handed it to his friend.

The first scene was a view of the car filled with mercenaries as it sped away from the location of the shooting attack.

"See if you can zoom in as close as you can to the car," Luke instructed.

"We'll wait for a good angle with a full view, then freeze the frame and print it."

"Got it," Leo acknowledged.

Right at the point where the car started to turn right at Ontario street and head in the direction of the Kennedy Expressway, Luke signaled for Leo to freeze the frame. Luke manipulated the image zoom features and stopped it when it focused in on a perfect top, right and rear side view of the car.

"Great picture," Luke announced.

"Let's print it."

Leo pressed the print button on the computer keyboard and instantly the photo was created.

"OK," Luke began.

"Now let's skip back to the airport and to the time when Samiha and I were getting into the taxi."
Leo pressed a few more buttons on the video remote and soon found the scene they were searching for. Luke and Samiha were just exiting the airport terminal and walking toward a waiting cab. Leo waited until he could get an unobstructed view of the two entering the car, then printed the image.

"Very good," Luke commented.
"Now we look for a good view of both our taxi and the shooter's car in close proximity. I want an obvious picture of them following us."
"Will do," Leo stated as he began to forward the scene in bursts of skips and pauses until he found the chance he liked.
Racing east along the expressway both vehicles were clearly visible with only several trucks and taxis separating them. Leo watched the screen carefully until the traffic began to slow at an area where other lanes merged, then he zoomed in and once again froze the frame and pressed the print button.

"That should be more than adequate in establishing the fact that you were being followed," Leo announced, as he touched the play button and resumed the action.
Soon the taxi exited at Ohio street with its pursuers not far behind. At LaSalle street they turned north and now Luke was visibly apprehensive as he moved closer to the edge of his seat and watched with renewed interest.

The chase vehicle suddenly bolted in a burst of speed and quickly overtook the taxi, as it came up to the right of it, only a few feet behind. Then flashes from weapon muzzles spewed out from the left rear window, shattering the taxi's rear glass, and filling the air with gun smoke.
In a quick move the taxi slammed to a screeching halt, then quickly turned about and fled back in the direction from where it came. The chaser hadn't anticipated the move and was forced to continue north, then turn right at the next intersection and head back to Ontario street .

Leo paused after printing three more photos of the attack and the taxi's escape.

"We've come full circle now," he said as he pressed the pause button.

Luke nodded.

"Yes. Now take it the other way. Go back to the scene of the airport and trace their steps. We'll need pictures of where they came from and what they were doing, or who they'd met with earlier in the day."

Leo complied and started the rewind sequence. He stopped it when they were able to spot the four shooters as they exited the airport terminal, some hours before, fresh off their flight into Chicago .

"So they are out-of-towners," Luke stated quietly.

"See if you can get a close up of their wrist watches. It would be useful to establish the exact time they arrived."

"Not a problem," Leo answered. After he printed several photos of the entire team he enhanced the image and successfully focused in on two of the men's left arms and the watches they wore.

"Almost three-o-clock," Leo announced.

"Yes," Luke acknowledged.

"Hours before our flight arrived and plenty of time for them to get prepared for us.

"Now follow them. Let's see where they go."

Leo tuned into the time when the four men were picking up a rental car and headed out of the airport area. They took a route north on the 294 toll way and exited not far away, at Touhy avenue . Several blocks down Touhy, they pulled into a parking lot behind a local cocktail lounge and stopped their car in the rear of building, out of sight from the street.

They appeared to be very familiar with the building as they exited the car and entered the building from a rear door.

"So this must be a contact spot for them," Luke said.

"No doubt this is where they picked up their guns since it's highly unlikely they were able to carry them on a commercial airliner, since they just got off a plane themselves."

"A safe assumption," Leo agreed.

"We'll get a photo of them coming out of the bar and then another few more when they return to the airport to wait for our arrival."

Leo kept the machine focused on the rear entrance until the four emerged. Then he zoomed in, froze the frame again and printed several photos. Back at the airport scene, now in the darkness of the early evening hours, the two watched the screen as their quarry circled the passengers arrival area several times. Leo paused the action several times to print more photos of their moving car as it passed through the airport streets.

"I think that should do it," Luke stated.

"We should have more than enough documentation on the airport activity for now. Let's go back to the bar and get a shot of them when they return. I'm really interested in other contacts they might have made."

Leo once again moved the image forward until the view returned them to a bird's eye view of the cocktail lounge. He moved the needle slightly and soon the scene they were looking for came into view.

First, an unfamiliar car pulled into the rear of the parking lot and came to rest near the back door of the building. Its occupant, a lone man dressed in a suit remained behind the wheel of his late model luxury car.

A few minutes passed before the rental car carrying the four mercenaries arrived and pulled in, parking next to the other vehicle.

"Try to get a close up of the other car's license plate or anything else we can use for positive identification," Luke suggested.

Leo nodded and waiting until all five men had exited their vehicles, then zoomed in for a clear close view.

"Oh my God!" Leo exclaimed.

"Those are Consulate Plates!"

"Really?" Can you make out the numbers?"

"No but the color is unmistakable and the window sticker in the right front windshield is clear as day. It's definitely a Consulate vehicle."

"Well we knew it had be something like that, I mean, someone in a high ranking political position, but now we know for sure," Luke attested.

He and Leo watched the screen in silence for a while as the five men huddled in conference. The man in the suit did not look pleased.

"These are some serious adversaries," Leo commented.

"And they have an air of authority about them that defies and intimidates, like they're untouchable."

"Yes," Luke agreed.

"All the more reason to keep them in check.

"Let's get a few group photos of this meeting, then tomorrow morning we'll trace this diplomat back to where he hangs his hat."

Leo clicked off a few more prints of the brief encounter then glanced over at Luke for a signal of what to do next.

"Let's call it a day," Luke announced.

"Tomorrow we'll find out a little more about that guy and what role he plays in all of this. I'm sure it will be very interesting."

"You go ahead," Leo suggested.

"Take the first room at the top of the stairs on the right. I'm gonna hang here a bit and satisfy a little curiosity."

"Suit yourself. It's your house. I'll see you in the morning."

Chapter Twenty

After Luke had left, Leo returned to his seat at the base of his sophisticated telescope and computer station. Looking at his wristwatch he made a few mental calculations that judged the current position and location of the satellite at this point in time, then began making a series of setting adjustments.
When he was reasonably satisfied, he switched on his massive customized viewing screen and set to the task of bringing into focus a specific image in a particular time.

At first, nothing was distinguishable except for a blurred view of rocky terrain but after a few clicks on his keyboard he finally arrived at the scene he desired, just above the furious activity of a new construction project. He had managed to navigate the Ocular's sights to the city Samiha's team had discovered, only now it was brand new and still undergoing the initial stages of construction and excavation.

Laborers scurried all about the area, digging footings, carrying water and materials, hammering forms and climbing in and out of newly dug holes in the ground. There were hundreds of workers, mostly clad only in white loin cloths and sun-blocking head gear. Only an occasional foreman or female water bearer could be seen fully attired.

Leo maneuvered the view with more clicks on his keyboard pad and kept the Ocular's focus in fine tune by holding the needle at its base steady. He scanned the entire work area and zoomed in for close up views on every individual in his line of vision for a long time before he eventually found what he was looking for. Then he saw him, standing alone along the outer ridge that over looked the entire construction site. It was the man Luke had recorded days earlier who had buried the Ocular beneath a door tract crevice so many thousands of years ago.

Leo gasped in awe. The tall man was fully clothed in white, angle length robes and a long white Kafir that he wore to protect his head. It was surrounded by a wide gold band that kept the headdress in place. Around his waist was a thick gold chain that was tied at his left side and hung loosely all the way down to his sandals.

His age appeared to be somewhere in the mid-thirties.
Leo zoomed in for a close clearer image and watched as the man walked slowly and carefully along the perimeter of the building site, about fifty yards away from the general activity.
Leo observed him for a long time, inwardly marveling at the man's impressive stature and carefree demeanor. After a while the man moved away from the ridge and walked toward a clearing off into the immediate distance, and toward a shady clearing where an open-air tent and small camp had been set up.
Leo recalled seeing this tent earlier, when Luke originally showed him the tapes he had recorded days before.

On the floor of the tent was the large tapestry rug upon which was decorated with the image of the Sun and the six planets that surrounded it, and the depiction of Venus on the day of Her birth as She speeded into Her new orbit following the Jupiter/Comet collision.
The man entered the tent briefly then soon emerged carrying another, large heavy folded colorful cloth. He opened it and laid it out onto the ground and stretched it out to expose its full twelve-foot square area. Leo moved his sights in closer to get a better view.
It was a map of the entire Earth, showing all the continents and oceans and other landmasses as well as many islands, some familiar to Leo and others strangely unrecognizable. He quickly pressed the print button on his keyboard to capture a perfect hard copy photo. The man then sat cross-legged on the ground next to the map and raised his eyes and arms toward the sky in an apparent gesture that suggested he knew he was being observed. Leo smiled as he wondered with amazement at the depth and vastness of this man's knowledge.

Leo continued to watch him as the man pointed to four distinct and separate spots on the map. He moved his finger slowly and deliberately first to one location, then to another just a fraction of an inch away, then to another, completely across to the other side of the map to an area Leo recognized as the North American continent, and specifically, to where what would now be the southwestern United States.

Leo surmised the location to be somewhere in upper Arizona . The fourth and final spot he pointed to, was the area now known as Peru , South America . Every point he touched with his fore finger was clearly marked with precise hairline crosses that were so fine in detail that they could only have been intended to indicate exact coordinates.

While Leo wondered about the meaning and significance of these marks the man once again raised his eyes and arms to the sky and smiled. Then he continued his pantomimic communication with a series of gestures that went on for about fifteen minutes. Leo realized that this person had anticipated the eventual discovery of the Time Ocular and was making every effort to relay to its future finders, details that he considered to be of importance.

Leo decided to freeze the moment and save it for future reference. He selected a blank video disc and inserted it into his CD burner, then scrolled back to the image of the moment when he first saw the man walking along the ridge. He then clicked a button on his keyboard and recorded the entire sequence. After a while the ancient traveler stopped his explanatory movements and settled into a cross-legged yoga like position, his hands resting on his knees and his eyes closed.

Leo watched him for a few more minutes until it because apparent that the man was prepared to remain in the meditating posture for some time to come. He removed the video disc and shut down the video equipment.

Samiha drew open the blinds of the bedroom windows, allowing a sudden splash of warm sunlight to spill over Luke's sleeping body. She leaned over him and delivered a gentle kiss near a corner of his mouth.

"Are you going to stay in bed all day?" she asked him, as his eyes fluttered open.
"What time is it?"
"Almost eleven," she answered. "Everyone else has been awake for hours."

Luke propped himself up onto one elbow and gazed quizzically through the open French windows that displayed a second story view of Leo's beautifully manicured garden below. Then he reached for Samiha's arm and gently drew her closer to himself. She sat on the edge of the bed next to him.

"Are you hungry?" She asked him.
"Yes. But not for bacon and eggs," he replied as he moved closer and kissed her passionately on the lips. She returned his kiss, then abruptly stood up and moved away from him.
"Come. We have much to do today," she told him. "I'll meet you back downstairs."

She winked at him before disappearing through the hall door. Luke showered and dressed quickly then rejoined his friends back in the observation room. "Where's Leo?" he asked after looking around the room and not seeing him.

Jess motioned for him to take a seat in front of the screen. "He's meeting Steve Sellser, the guy from WTTW TV right now as we speak."
"Already? I'd think it's still too early for that," Luke remarked.
"You won't think so after you have a look at the most recent tapes Leo put together this morning."
"Doesn't that guy get any sleep?"
"I asked him the same question," Jess replied. "He's been up since six-o'clock. Apparently five hours a day is all he needs."

Jess handed him the remote control unit.

"Turn it on. It's all been set, ready for you to see. Leo and I went over it together this morning."

Luke clicked on the screen and pressed the play button. At once it displayed a view of a very populated city, and from the indications of street signs and billboards it was obviously a city somewhere in the United States.

Crowds of people flanked the sidewalks that lined a stretch of a main street. As his friends watched, Jess explained.
"Do you remember when that Arabian King visited Dallas , Texas a few years ago, and was shot while riding in a motorcade with some local politicians?"
Luke nodded. "Of course. How could I forget? It was top news for weeks."
"Right," Jess acknowledged and went on.
"Certain elements claimed that it was a well organized conspiracy, while most contended that it was the work of a lone assassin, and even later an investigation commission determined that one man, acting alone... a supposed fanatic... was responsible for the shooting."
"I recall it well," Luke said. "I followed the story all along."
"Well that's not what happened," Jess announced. "You're about to witness the entire event live and in living color. Keep watching. This gets very interesting."

Samiha joined Luke on the couch and handed him a fresh steaming cup of coffee. Although she had already seen the tape earlier that morning, while Leo Jess mulled over it, her apprehension was very apparent by her nervousness as she looked at the screen.

"This is the actual assassination?" Luke asked loudly with surprise. Jess just looked at him somberly and nodded.
From the angle of vision the telescope focused in on a parade of colorfully flagged limousines that moved slowly in a procession toward the forefront.

Armed police and plain clothed escorts jogged in step on either side of the vehicles while interested spectators smiled and waved as they passed.

"Now watch that clump of grassy knoll just on the right," Jess instructed.
He had barely finished speaking when a small but distinguishable puff of gray smoke accompanied with a sleek flash of fire burst from deep within the thickness of the tall grass.

"Freeze the frame," Jess said, then pointed to a drainage sewer built into the side of the street's curb directly across from the grassy area. Luke stopped the video action momentarily, then pressed the play button once again when his attention was prepared.
Another quick blast of smoke and flame loomed out from behind the steel drainage grid, almost simultaneously with the first gun shot.
Jess then directed attention to a third location.

"Now look at the upper window in that book building down the street." Again, and for the third time another brief but unmistakable sputter of fire and smoke occurred. Instant pandemonium took over the crowds. All eyes were immediately glued to the King's limousine as the body of the Royal jerked violently, first in a slight forward slump, then slammed backward as if kicked in the forehead by a full grown mule.

Blood and body parts splattered the across the trunk of the long black car and other occupants threw themselves on the floor. Samiha covered her face with her hands at the horrific sight while Luke was frozen in astonishment. No one said a word for a while as the tape continued to run for few minutes longer until it skipped to resume at another scene.

Jess explained, "Leo omitted a lot of the footage that wasn't really necessary. He wanted to edit only the important sights.

This is several minutes later after the motorcade has sped off. Watch the front entrance of that book building now."
Luke watched as he was instructed and very soon a figure emerged from the front door. Dressed in business attire and carrying an inconspicuous briefcase was a man Luke recognized immediately.
"That's one of the guys who followed us and shot me!"
"Yep," Jess agreed, "and two of his buddies are there too."
The scene skipped again to the area of the tall grass, at the moment only seconds after the gun smoke had dissipated in the wind. The close-up showed a man to be quickly disassembling a snipers rifle and scope, and packing it away inside a workman's toolbox.
He then strolled briskly down the shallow hill away from his vantage point to a waiting car about a hundred yards away. No one noticed him or his partner who greeted him at the car and opened the trunk into which the toolbox was dropped. Within a few short minutes they were speeding away.

"You're correct," Luke acknowledged. "I don't recognize the driver, but there's no mistaking the other guy. He was one of them too."
The tape skipped once more to the area of the sewer's drainage grid, where a third assassin had laid in ambush.

"There's a rain tunnel that runs along under the street," Jess explained, "and spills out into a main waterway that opens up about a quarter mile away under that bridge."

Jess pointed to the structure as the scene moved in closer to focus in on the drainage opening he had referred to. Under the bridge, directly beneath the viaduct and over looking the river, a figure of a man appeared as he scurried out of the tunnel and dropped down into the shallow waters at the river's edge. Cautiously he scanned the immediate area for signs of life then scampered up the embankment to a car that had been parked along side the road, just a few feet down from the bridge.

Luke remembered his face from the tape that recorded both, the airport and parking lot scenes. He carried what appeared to be a dark overnight case as he hurried to the car and soon disappeared down the road in the direction of the interstate highway.
Luke slumped back into his seat shaking his head in disgust.

"Unbelievable," he uttered. "But I don't understand. How did they happen to accuse and convict the sole gunman? I was under the impression that this was an open and shut case against the guy. Hell, the entire world was convinced that he was the only person responsible for the shooting!"
"He was set up," Jess announced. "A perfect patsy for a perfectly executed assassination by individuals and for reasons that they could not permit to be exposed. For a killing like this they needed a fall guy, someone to pin it on, to throw off all possibility of detection with a story so believable that it would be accepted and redirect any suspicion away from the actual motives."
"How do you know all of this?" Luke asked him.
"Keep watching the tape. There's more." They continued to view the screen as it displayed another image of a young man in his mid twenties, as he stood in the doorway of the book building watching the motorcade as it passed him, while drinking a can of Coke.
"That's the man who was accused!"
"Yes," Luke agreed. "I recognize his face from the photos in the news."
Jess continued,
"Leo traced his movements from this moment, back to several weeks in the past, where the next few scenes show him talking with one of the actual shooters on several different occasions. The latest meeting occurred only a couple of days before the day of the assassination."

Luke watched as the tape skipped several times to scenes of the meetings as Jess described.
"We can't know what the conversations were about." Jess went on, "But the implications are as obvious as the nose on your face. They used him. They played him like a grand piano!"

Luke nodded in agreement. "So it appears. Well this certainly changes everything. We seem to be holding all of the trump cards now."

"And it explains why they want you dead and the Ocular in their possession. The people that hired them know what it can do because they have one of their own."

"God forbid!" Samiha shuttered at the thought. "If they knew what evidence we had now, every one of us would be killed."

"That's for sure," Jess remarked. So you see why Leo felt that it is important for us to move very quickly. He also discussed the possibility of going to the authorities, but we all agreed that we couldn't trust that option. Which 'authority' would we select to go to? And what if some of our own enforcers of the law were involved in some way? If we made the wrong decision it would be like walking right into the jaws of the lion.

"The best authority, we also agreed to be, are the people who were lied to, duped by this outrageous criminal act, perpetrated by selfish and immoral motives, then covered up with more lies.

"This really pisses me off, the more I think about it," Jess rambled on. "They've not only committed cold blooded murder, but they've set into motion a continuance of their fabricated mistruths to be stuffed down the throats of history students for generations to come.

"So I think that the best plan is your original one. To take it to the people through an objective media like we discussed. That's the very best thing we can do."

Luke nodded. "And probably the safest too. Not that it's never been attempted before when conspiracies were exposed, but we have an edge. We have pictures. Which brings us to another important issue; one that our friend Judy of the FBI touched briefly on when I called her as she was about to follow those guys into my building."

"What's that?" Jess asked him.

"The act of exposing something to the people of this country that might set off a chain reaction of revolt or widespread unrest accompanied with more distrust, or at the very least, a lot of painful emotion.

"Let's think about this for a minute. Let's assume that the foreign government who now has in their possession, the original Ocular found in the Sodieum Cave, also has a collection of tapes or pictures not unlike the ones we've created these past few days. We'd have to be idiots to assume they didn't. There's absolutely no doubt in my own mind that they do.

"Let's further assume on these tapes of theirs are records of events of similar atrocities committed by our own government or agencies affiliated with it. Those records would be terrific trump cards of their own to use as they pleased to negotiate things they wanted in return for keeping silent."

"What would be unleashed if, because of us, these events and records were also made public?"

Jess shrugged his shoulders.

"I should think that no matter how horrible, the truth should come out. People deserve the truth."

"You say that now," Luke said, "but I wonder if the truth wouldn't do irreparable damage to a lot of innocent people."

"So what else could we do?" Jess asked him.

Luke pondered his question for a moment before replying. "We play a little poker with these guys. We continue to follow up with the idea to use Steve Seller's TV show and leak only a few details... not everything for now... but in the meantime we devise a plan to meet with that diplomat boss of theirs and arrange a deal."

"A deal?" Samiha echoed. "What kind of deal?"

Luke shook his head. "I don't know yet. But I'll come up with something."

☙

Chapter Twenty One

In her supervisor's office Judy was shocked when she came face to face again with the four men she had stopped outside of Luke's building the other day. They had been there for a while, in conference with her boss and two other high ranking officials, also with the FBI. Both of them stood like soldiers, against one wall of the large office, their arms folded as they studied Judy and Michael when the two entered.

Her mood turned suddenly reserved as she and her partner were directed to take seats near the four men.

"This is an informal meeting," one of the officials began. "You've been asked to join us here today for two reasons. Number one, to inform you that you two are being reassigned. There's to be no more contact or supervision between you and your archeologist friends. We're taking over the entire matter from here on out."

"What's going on?" Judy interrupted. "Why pull us off the case now?"

"I'm sorry about this," her boss submitted. "It's all news to me too." The official ignored them both and continued.

"And number two, to explain to you that these matters are touching upon issues of high priority that are classified Top Secret, which we and these four guests of ours are currently involved with.

"There's absolutely no reflection on your own performance or abilities. It's just that we're forced to keep a tighter rein on all persons allowed to be directly involved with this situation."

"I see," Judy commented. Michael remained silent, sitting very still at her side.

The 'four guests' appeared to be very relaxed with an air of indifference and mild tolerance. One of the men moved slightly to the edge of his seat and leaned toward them before he spoke with a hint of ethnic accent.

"But you can still help us," he stated. "We would appreciate it if you could shed some light on a few details for us; possibly provide us with any information on their other friends and especially their current whereabouts. Anything you can share with us will help."

Judy looked at him as he spoke but purposely ignored him and turned away to face her boss, who had still not established eye contact with her.

"We can't be sure," she answered. "In fact we don't know. Luke Ozman and his assistant haven't returned to his condo since the day after their arrival from the Middle East . I've spoken to him by phone only once since then."

"You have? When?" the official asked her.

Judy did a great job of camouflaging her feelings of distain.

"It was the same day we first encountered these men, right outside Luke's building. We'd been watching his front entrance that afternoon when he called me. He was concerned for the safety of his assistant and himself and asked if we'd made any progress with finding out about the people that followed them from the airport and shot at their taxi."

One of the four men fidgeted nervously for a brief instant while another cleared his throat. Michael and Judy exchanged meaningful glances and she continued.

"I informed him that it was imperative that he meet with us. He refused. He told me that he would not meet or even disclose his location. He did promise to get back with me later, however."

"And that's all he said?" the official asked her. "Nothing more?"

"No sir."

Michael didn't speak with her until they were well away from the office and walking back toward their car.

"You didn't tell them everything back there. Why?" he asked.

"Because I don't like those guys. I don't like anything about this whole thing. Just the thought that we're in cahoots with people like that makes every inch of my red-blooded American skin crawl!"

She was visibly shaken and angry as they got back into their vehicle.

"Here's a team of hired killers, in our country, walking around nonchalantly with Cart Blanc to run rampant through our neighborhoods, doing exactly as they please. What's going on here? What are we doing with these people and why?"

"I understand how you feel, Judy," Michael muttered half-heartedly, "but we can't very well fight City Hall on this one. It's too big for us."

Judy exhaled a sigh of indignation.

"I know. That's what bothers me the most!"

"You and I both know that those archeologists are completely innocent of any wrong doing whatsoever, and guilty only of making worthwhile contributions to education, science and to the people of this country to whom we are sworn to protect at all costs."

"So they found this fantastic machine that can perform all of these strange and super feats. So what? Why does that fact have everyone worried and acting as if the world's coming to an end? Why are we forced to turn a blind eye to a team of thugs whose only objective is to kill honest citizens and steal for themselves, something they'd probably use for no good anyway?"

Michael nodded. "I'm on your side partner. But our hands are tied. Aside from the minor detail that the FBI signs our paychecks, it's obvious that this guy Luke and his friends have managed to stumble onto something that reaches all the way up to the top. And we're definitely in no position to buck the bosses."

Judy looked into her friend's eyes for a moment before she spoke again.

"Well I don't care. Just between you and I, we have to find a way to get a message to them. They're in more danger now than they ever were."

When Leo returned in the early afternoon from his rendezvous with Steve Sellser at WTTW, he was excited.
"It turned out to be a very productive meeting," he announced to his friends as they greeted him at the front door.

"I just hope you didn't tell him *too* much," Luke commented.
"Oh no," Leo replied. "Just enough to tweak his interest and certainly nothing about the Time Ocular at all.

"Did you look at the tapes Jess and I put together this morning?"
"I did," Luke replied. "Great stuff. Just what we needed.
"What did your connection at the TV station have to say?"
Leo gave him one of his wide beaming smiles. "He was really impressed. I took him a few of the photos you and I printed up last night and I showed him this."
Leo removed a folded dishcloth from his sport jacket pocket and opened it to reveal the stone carved image of the planets Samiha's digger had found.
"Good," Luke acknowledged. "What photos did you let him see?"
"Just three. The ones that showed them following your taxi from the airport, the one we took when they were behind you on the expressway on your way into the city, and one where you and Samiha are getting into the cab when you arrived. Steve is working on a piece right now that he'll have ready for tonight around nine o'clock."
"Really?" Samiha asked him. "We'll be on television tonight?"
"Yes.... well, just the photos and a picture of the stone carving. What I did was wet his appetite with a promise that he'd get the exclusive on the entire story when the time was right. He's only

gonna do a bit that'll air no more than thirty seconds or so, but it'll be an interesting delivery. He'll ask some things that will raise questions about why these people are so stirred over your discovery. If nothing else, his documentary will send a message to these killers that you, (we) know how to use the Ocular and it'll also establish a concrete record with the media."

"And what about Steve Sellser?" Jess inquired with clear concern in his tone. "Here's yet another person who's life we're putting in danger."

"I warned him about that possibility as best I could without divulging too much. I told him that we had no idea to what lengths these characters would stretch to get what they were after. He just laughed at me. He's convinced that he isn't worried about any possible threat to him or the station. Media types love that kind of drama anyway. And although I emphasized with him that none of us can possibly be aware of the actual degree of potential danger, he insisted that he was well protected against that kind of thing."

"Maybe so," Luke mumbled, "but if they can get to *him*, they can find us."

"That's why we have to move quickly, Luke," Leo contended. "The sooner we're able to create enough objective interest from the public, and especially the scientific world, where that TV station reaches most, the sooner we'll be able to enjoy a reasonable degree of safety for ourselves.

"Don't forget," Leo went on, "they have an Ocular too. And whatever we can do, they can probably do better."

"Good point," Luke admitted. "Another important reason for why we should be looking in on that diplomat connection of theirs, and right now. In fact, from this point on, we should be keeping a continued surveillance on him."

Leo nodded in agreement. "So let's do it," he said.

Back in the observation room Leo went right to work on calibrating the settings he needed to tune back to the time of the initial meeting of the five men, behind the cocktail lounge, in the parking lot. He zoomed in on the Consulate's vehicle parked next to the four shooter's rental car, then moved the image even closer as the man exited. This time, Leo sharpened up a clearer focus on the man's face, as best he could. "Well that's our guy," he said as he moved in even closer. "OK. Now I'll bring the total image back until we have a bird's eye view of the entire area so I can follow him."

He adjusted the sights and angle of vision until it had zoomed out to a distance he was comfortable with. Now it appeared that they were watching them from the top of an eight-story building. "Perfect. Now we'll see where this bastard came from." Leo announced as he began to move the sensitive needle along the base of the Ocular with one hand while clicking arrow buttons on his keyboard with the other.

He started the rewind effect and they all watched in silence for a while as the car appeared to move backwards through busy traffic and the streets of Chicago .
The trace eventually ended in the downtown area, at the Civic Center 's parking garage entrance.

"Damn," Leo muttered. "That's a big place to have to search. There must be thousands of cars and just as many offices in that building."
"Freeze the frame right now, before the car backs up into the garage," Luke told him. Leo did as instructed then zoomed in to bring the vehicle into a close-up view.

"Now focus in on that parking sticker on his windshield."
Leo tapped a button on the keyboard a few times until the image of the window sticker cleared up and became visible enough to read the name and serial numbers printed across its face. "That's an Israeli Consulate parking sticker," Luke announced. "Now we know what office to look for. All we hafta do now is attach a name to the face. One of us needs to get over there and check it out.

"Jess, you should go. Samiha and I are too recognizable and none of these people have seen you yet. Get down there, look up the office directory and find out that guy's name. As soon as you have it, call us from there right away. Are you up for this?"
Jess didn't hesitate. "Absolutely! I'll go right now."
Samiha grabbed his arm. "Please be careful," she insisted, as he quickly left the room.
"We'll be watching for you from here." Leo said to him.

Leo restarted the play sequence then moved the telescope's position to view the main area of the Civic Center's many entrance doors. Except for the late evening hours it was always a very busy courtyard. Hundreds of people hurried about, keeping the turn-styles of the entrance ways constantly in motion, with visitors, and employees of every conceivable state, local or federal agency. Tourists flocked from all over the world here, to photograph or just enjoy one of Picasso's massive landmark works of art that occupied much of the center of the courtyard area.

Leo had stopped using the Ocular for the time being and now the screen filled with the bustling activity of the present time.
The three of them continued to watch for about twenty minutes, until Jess's familiar figure could be seen walking briskly toward the front of the building. He paused momentarily to glance up at the sky, then disappeared into the building. "Too bad the ocular can't see through steel buildings," Leo commented.

"I'm still amazed by what it *can* see," Luke offered. "But that's a good point," he continued. "I'm sure that some planetary obstructions occasionally block the line of vision of the 'Hubbles' that connect the ocular's receiver."
Leo shook his head in disagreement.

"That kind of comparison doesn't apply," he said with solid conviction. "First of all any obstruction of a planetary nature would probably be less apparent than a flea on a full blown movie screen, if only for the vast distances involved. And second,

if your theory on multiple Hubbles is correct, and I'm convinced
it is, then our Ocular receives very much like several different
cameras set up around various positions around a baseball field
when telecasting a game. When one view is temporarily blocked,
another kicks in creating the illusion of constancy, shifting from
one angle of sight to another."
Luke nodded in agreement. "I'm sure your right. Still, it's all
amazing to me."

Only a few more minutes passed before Leo's telephone rang.
Leo answered it and was silent then scribbled something on a
note pad.
"OK. Get back here as fast as you can," he said. "That was Jess.
The guy's name is Seymore Burnstien. According to Jess he's the
senior advisor to the Israeli ambassador."
"He's sure about that?" Luke asked him, somewhat surprised.
Leo nodded. "He sounded pretty convinced to me."

Luke shook his head in distain. "We knew we were up against
some major players, but this takes the cake."
"I'm not at all surprised," Samiha blurted. "I've been educated
here and spent most of my young life in schools while in this
country, but one only needs to watch the evening news, on any of
the big three networks, to realize it is anything but objective.
"My people are always depicted as the bad guys, when if the real
truth were known, both sides of the issues, the people of the
United States wouldn't stand for it one more minute."
"This isn't about 'sides' or 'issues'," Luke replied sternly. "It's
not about what this Aborigine thinks or that Christian or Jew
believes. That's been a major problem with worldly differences
ever since governments were established. We tend to feed on the
embellishments of who's right and who's wrong, on whom to
blame and who to exonerate. It becomes easier to fight among
one another when we look a little different, or practice beliefs
that are strange to others.

"This is the Earth. On Earth there is only one human race. And
like it or not, the world we created is saturated with fundamental

ideology that I'm right and you're wrong. It's that very hodgepodge of justifiable grievance that keeps us identified with bickering. We need someone to attack, someone to blame."

"Sure," Samiha muttered almost inaudibly. "Too bad everyone doesn't think like you, Luke," she said as she left the room.

Judy was home mixing a glass of iced tea when her phone rang. Her partner's voice crackled with urgency as he shouted from the other ended of the line.

"Judy, turn on your TV to channel eleven right now!"
"What is it?" she asked calmly.
"Hurry up!" he demanded. "Turn it on now."
Judy clicked on her small kitchen counter set and flipped it to set the channel to eleven. At the sight of the picture of the stone carving, her mouth dropped open in surprise. She recalled their initial meeting at Luke's home, the day after the shooting attack, and how Luke and Samiha had shown her the discovery.
"Are you still there?" Michael barked into her ear, with more urgency.

"I'm here. Be quiet a minute. I want to hear this."
Steve Selser narrated:
"Our archeologist friends at the Loyola University , here in Chicago, who we rely on for up-to-date information related to new or current events in the world of discovery, have graciously shared this exciting new development.

"Just South of the site of the Great Pyramids in Egypt , this baffling artifact was excavated from the depths of a recently uncovered city that was built to house workers many thousands of years ago.

"Beneath an ancient door track, buried some twenty-five thousand years ago, Samiha Salaha and her crew dug up what appears to be this engraved drawing of some of the planets in our solar system, some of which, I might add, that had not technically been discovered until much later.

"But what's even more baffling is the strange behavior of a group of unidentified individuals who were photographed as they followed Luke Ozman, of the University, as he accompanied Miss Salaha after their arrival at O'Hare Airport.

"Here are the three photos we were able to use.
"Our question is why all the interest in these two well known and highly respected scientists who have served our interests many times in the past? Who are these people and why are following them?
"We don't know all of the details right now, but we've been assured that we'll be kept up on future developments, which we will pass on to you as they unfold." His narration continued onto another subject.

Judy was impressed. "That son of a gun!" she exclaimed. "Luke let on that he would do something like this."
"Well, he wasn't bluffing," Michael commented.
Judy's mind raced as she mentally evaluated the new development, then had another idea.

"When you hang up with me, put a call into the office and leave an urgent message to have the Chief call you back as soon as possible. When he does, fill him in on the TV show, if he doesn't already know about it. I want them all to be aware of it. Try to feel out what his evaluation is, but be discreet, then call me back here as soon as you've heard from him."
"Will do," Michael replied. "What are you gonna do?" he asked.
"I'm going to try to reach that Steve Selser guy at the TV station. Maybe I'll be able to get a message to Luke Ozman and his friends through him.

"I wonder if they realize what they've done. They just lit a fire under the ass of a hungry tiger. I hope for Luke's sake, he knows what he's doing."

&

Chapter Twenty Two

The two white robed comrades strolled the dig site well into the night as they continued to exchange thoughts. The elder was speaking.

"Our brethren are hampered in their progress by their demands to know what they do not know. This is actually a way of hanging on to deprivation. One cannot reasonably object to following instructions in a course for knowing, on the grounds that you do not know. The need for the course is implicit in your objection. Knowledge is not the motivation for learning this... Peace is. As the *prerequisite* for knowledge, peace must be learned. This is only because those who are in conflict are not peaceful, and peace is the *condition* of knowledge because it is the condition of the their true 'home'.

Knowledge will be restored when they meet its conditions. This is not a bargain made by *Source*, who made no bargains at all. It is merely the result of your misuse of *Source's* Laws on behalf of a will that was not of *Source*. Knowledge is *Source's* Will. If you are opposing that will, how can you have knowledge?

What knowledge offers you is clear, but it is also clear that they do not regard this as wholly desirable. If they did, they would hardly be willing to throw it away so readily, when the ego asks for their allegiance.

The distraction of the ego seems to interfere with learning, but it has no power to distract unless given it the power. The ego's voice is an hallucination. You cannot expect the ego to say "I am not real." Hallucinations are inaccurate perceptions of reality. But our brethren are not asked to dispel them alone. They are merely asked to evaluate them in terms of their results to them. If they do not want them on the basis of loss of peace, they will be removed from their mind *for* them. Every response to the ego is a call to war, and war *does* deprive one of peace.

Yet in this war their is no opponent. *This* is the reinterpretation of reality which one must make to secure peace, and the only one our brethren need ever make. Those whom one perceives as opponents are *part* of their peace, which he is giving up by attacking them. How can you have what YOU give up? You share to have, but you do not give it up yourselves. When you give up peace, you are excluding yourself from it. This is a condition which is so alien to the realm of *Source* that one cannot understand the state which prevails within it.

"I understand," the younger offered, and he went on, "But they're doing the best that they can, given their current condition of their blindness to true perception. As you pointed out earlier there are those among them, writers, authors, speakers, teachers and even those in seclusion whose very presence emanates a balance of integrous intention. They know *Source*. They live within it as do we, and with experience their entire worldly collective will rise above their murky fog of blindness and achieve the state of oneness that is their heritage."

"Yes." The elder agreed.
"They will. In the meantime, this new found treasure of theirs, this *Time Ocular* as they have already coined it, will serve as just another one of their sharp edged toys with which to exact their continued validation with the world of form. They will use until, as we did, eventually see its senseless. "

∂

I've figured out a what kind of deal I can present to these rats," Luke told Leo as the two of them looked through the stack of photos they had comprised.

"What's that?" Leo asked him.
Luke looked weary and tired. The past few days had obviously taken a toll on him. He spoke slowly and carefully, with resigned conviction for what he was about to announce.

"The Time Ocular shouldn't be in the hands of anyone, either our government or theirs. The world just isn't ready for it. The power it can unleash is too terrible and the damage it can cause, the lives it can disrupt, far outweighs the benefits."
"What are you saying, Luke? One government already has an Ocular in their possession. There's nothing you or any of us can do about that."
"It might appear that way." Luke replied,
"But I have an idea that might make it possible to remove it from them."
Samiha joined them just then and sat down to listen.
"We already know that it's all too possible that besides having an Ocular in their possession, they also have damning material they created with it designed for only one purpose. To blackmail or harm people if exposed."
"Granted," Leo agreed.
"Go on."
"Who can say what they really have. Probably some really damning stuff. Just from the brief experience we've had over the past few days, and the information we compiled in that relatively short period of time should tell us that they have had much more time to experiment with it, and God only knows how they've used it.
"So what I propose is two things. One, we make available the tapes we put together on the assassination to our government through the FBI. That'll create a stalemate effect for both sides.

Each will have something on the other. A little like a cold war chess game."

"Makes sense," Leo commented.

"What's the other thing?"

"We let them know that we'll destroy everything we've recorded on the condition that they destroy their Ocular, and even offer to do the same with our own if that's what it takes."

Leo starred at his friend in total disbelief. Samiha was equally stunned.

Luke went on,

"I just don't see any other solution. You said yourself, Leo, and I agree, we must move quickly on this. If we remain in the same situation for very much longer, it'll only be a matter of time before the powers that be come crashing down around our heads. They'll kill us, either one side or the other and in the end, nothing will have been accomplished!

"Yeah, maybe there would be an out-cry if something happened to me or Samiha or any of us, and there would be investigations. Questions would be asked and some sacrificial lambs would be offered up to take the blame, but when the smoke cleared and time passed, we'd still be very dead and the Ocular will remain in the hands of authorities who couldn't care less."

Leo let out a long sigh of disappointment. He shook his head in disgust when he said, "There's gotta be another way, Luke. I can't accept having to forfeit the absolute find of all finds....," his voice trailed off.

"Are you sure, Luke?" Samiha begged.

"Are you absolutely sure you want to do this? Maybe we can disappear, leave here and go somewhere with the Ocular..."

"And what?" Luke interrupted.

"Think about what you're saying. How long do you suppose we could run and hide before they finally put their own Ocular to use against us? And what kind of life would that be, for you or me? What of our friends here? Would we leave them to the mercy of murderous scum who have already killed other friends of ours,

and would not think twice of doing it again so long as it served
their own purposes?
"I can see no other alternative."

"Listen Luke," Leo began with a firmness unusual in his
generally gentle nature. "You said yourself that we should fight
fire with fire and let them know that *we know*. Before you make
this drastic decision give me a little time to come up with another
solution. Just a few hours, maybe until tomorrow morning. If I
have to, I'll work on it all night."
"I'm listening. What do you have in mind?" Luke asked him.
Leo wrung his big hands together and looked around the room
before answering.
"Luke, this discovery of yours is far too important to throw away
or even compromise. Not when it promises to be a wealth of
potential knowledge for future research. We cannot allow the
actions of a few social misfits to dictate a course of action as you
suggest, no matter how far up the ladder of authority they reach.
"I want to do a little more digging on past meetings and
conversations between highest level figures in political power, on
both sides. Maybe we can get lucky and find something that can
help us."

Luke lightly touched the bandaged wound on his neck and
thought about Leo's words for a moment. Then he shook his
head.
"Don't you think that these high level political shysters have
thought about the possibility that someone would try to
eavesdrop on them? Don't you realize that they've undoubtedly
taken every precaution against that sort of thing? What do you
believe you can accomplish by peeking in on them with the Time
Ocular? It's been tried before by every camera buff on the
planet!"
Leo would not be discouraged.

"We don't know if it'll work or what we'll stumble upon unless
we try," he stated. "Like I said, Luke, maybe we can get lucky.

"Not long ago I read a rather lengthy article in one of the national news magazines that talked about the practice of using doubles and stand-ins. Top political leaders very often use them to take their place during certain public appearances, so while it appears that they're kissing babies and shaking hands on one side the country, they're really somewhere else, doing other things, miles away.

"The public is fooled and they're temporarily doing things that will never be recorded in their official activities."
Luke smiled. "I never thought about that."
"It's very true," Leo continued, "and probably happens more often than we've ever suspect."
"So what you're suggesting," Luke asked, "is that you might be able to catch them in the act of being somewhere they're not supposed to be? And maybe during one of these unrecorded events, look in on some special meeting of the minds at some remote fishing hole?"
"Exactly!" Leo confirmed.
"It's very possible. A fishing hole we can zoom in on and not be restricted by the normal security they're used to using when conducting an actual appearance. If they've done it time and time again, it's very likely they'd be comfortable and relaxed in the situation and might tend to leave most of their usual guard down. Maybe we could get very lucky and find something really crucial and juicy."
"Anything's possible I suppose," Luke commented, not totally convinced, "but you'd still be searching for a needle in a haystack. A long shot at best. Do you have any ideas on where you'd start looking?"

Leo thought about it for a minute then replied,
"I could go on line and search through recent newspaper articles that announced public appearances, or special events that were attended by top figureheads. Once I've accumulated enough potential dates and times I can start a trace with the Ocular and hopefully land on just one good, solid event that could be just what we need."

Luke nodded.

 "OK. Try it out."

❧

Chapter Twenty Three

A special meeting was suddenly called at FBI headquarters. This time, Judy and her partner were not invited. Their chief supervisor sat in with his two bosses and only one of the four special "guests" they had met with earlier.

The atmosphere in the room was tense and highly irritated.

"How could we have allowed this to get so far out of hand?" shouted one of the officials. "Now they're on television with this shit?"

The chief threw an ugly glare at the leader of the shooter's team. "If nitwit here and his team hadn't screwed it up from the beginning we wouldn't be talking right now."

"Look," the assassin began, "we'll deal with this. It's not the first time we've had a problem or two."

"Wrong! This problem is unique!" barked the official.

"This time they have pictures! And pictures can't be undone!

"Unless we get to them now, and I mean *now*, everybody's ass is on the line! Do you realize what they can do to us?"

The leader of the shooters waved his hand in dismissal.

"Relax. I finally weeded through all the red tape and got authorization to use our machine to track them down. There was a lot of red tape involved, and until the guys upstairs realized the gravity of the situation, it was impossible to get them to approve it.

"Now that they understand that there's another Time Viewing Machine involved, and in the hands of people that shouldn't have it, they agreed immediately. Even as we speak there's a spy plane on the way."

"Well I'd say it was about time," the chief uttered sarcastically and he went on.

"We all knew, from the beginning, that these archeologists were not just some group of inconsequential citizens. We knew they'd make some noise. You should've taken them out in your own back yard."

"We didn't have all of the details then!" he retorted. "We knew absolutely nothing until we talked with that project manager of theirs. How could we have known what they found?"

"Yeah, but when you did know, you bungled the opportunity. You turned the city of Chicago into the a wild west show and managed to set into motion one of the biggest fiascos we've ever been faced with."

One of the officials rose from his chair and stood directly in front of the shooter's team leader.

"Listen to me," he began with a tone that indicated boiling rage. "We've gone along with you guys for years now, partly because we had no choice.

"You've had us over a barrel for a long time. And we accepted it. You've been paid billions of dollars, been granted free passes to do exactly as you pleased with your own territorial problems, we've given unlimited support, arms, clout and anything you needed.

"We've let you blackmail us for long enough! So you know what we're gonna do now? We're gonna go after this group of archeologists ourselves, and we're gonna get that machine of theirs, and when we have it, all bets are off. 'cuz I'm gambling that you guys don't want us having that thing any more than we enjoy the knowledge that *you* have one."

The shooter glared at him for a moment then calmly said, "Don't threaten me. I'm the last guy in the world that you wanna mess with."

The chief quickly came from around his desk and separated the two, moving his boss over to a corner of the room.

"Fighting among ourselves isn't going to solve anything," he said.

"We have a situation here that needs our full, undivided cooperation."

The shooter pointed his finger in their direction and raised his voice.

"Just remember one thing. If I think for an instant, that you or any of your people are entertaining the thought of turning against us, woe be unto you. Your entire country will be thrown into instant upheaval. Your patriots will be burning down your Capital Building by tomorrow."

"Just cool off," the chief told him.

"Both of you! The very last thing we need right now is dissention between us!"

The chief looked at his boss with urgent eyes that begged for compromise. The other sat back down in his chair and didn't say another word.

"This spy plane that's on the way," the other official began, "when is it due and what are your plans for it?"

"We expect check-in contact from the pilot by tomorrow morning, following final refueling," he replied and continued. "We'll be directing its movements from here, sending it to the last know location of the archeologists, and in a matter of a few minutes we'll have pin pointed where they've set up housekeeping. Once we know, we'll have them. There's absolutely no way they can hide."

"Thank God you called me back," Judy told Luke.

"I managed to convince your friend at channel eleven to get my message to you."

"Yes," Luke answered her. "He just hung up with one of my associates. He said that you sounded very concerned and that you were super persistent. What's the problem?"

Judy's tone of voice was extremely urgent.

"Luke, I'm gonna speak to you as one human being to another who cares for doing the right thing, like a friend, I hope, who doesn't want to see another get hurt."
Luke was moved by here sincerity and compassion.
"I appreciate that. Thank you. I'd like to consider you a friend. Please go on."
"You and your partners are in grave danger!" she blurted out.
"During the past few days I've witnessed things and been in the company of people who frankly, turn my stomach when I think about what they're up with regard to you and your newest archeological discovery.
"I don't mind admitting to you that I am ashamed of some of my own peers, including my boss and some other higher ups that I work for, who are engaged in secret dealing with the very people who shot you.

"I do not condone their actions nor do I agree with them, and I thought it best to warn you, that they may soon take measures that will put your life and the lives of anyone you are directly involved with, in serious jeopardy."
Samiha, Leo and Jess watched Luke as he closed his eyes and rubbed his forehead with one hand, while holding the cell phone to his ear with the other. He seated himself at Samiha's side before he spoke.

"Judy, I'm very aware of the gravity of the situation and I also know exactly who we are dealing with, and how powerful they are. You are not stupid by any means, and this phone call only confirms for me, that you are just as knowledgeable as anyone, about what's really going on here.

"We have something they want very badly and the very saddest thing about it all, the most disheartening factor, is that members of my own government's law enforcement agencies are just as corrupt and underhanded as any bad guy can be."
"We're not all bad guys, Luke," she said softly, almost whispering.

"I know that. It's just a shame that the ones who are, happen to be the powers that pull all the strings."

Luke's friends listened attentively as the conversation continued. "I want to help you, if I can," Judy offered.
"Whatever I can do that won't jeopardize my partner or his livelihood, or safety... anything within reason. I want you to feel free to call me anytime, day or night, and in the meantime, wherever you are, stay hidden. Don't venture out for anything."
"Your kindness is refreshing, Judy. It's good to know that you're on my side.
"I've given a lot of thought to how I'll resolve this dilemma, and I'm very close to bringing this situation to a close."
"What will you do?"
"I won't go into details right now, but I'll tell you this; my main concern is for the safety of my friends and myself, and although the scientist in me wants to preserve, at all costs, the amazing find we have stumbled upon, I'll give up the machine in a minute, if it comes to that, and if it means choosing between it and the security of the people close to me.
"Whatever happens, and whatever I decide to do, you'll be one of the first to know about it.
"I'm grateful to you, more than you know, for the offer to help."
"Well, don't even hesitate to call me for anything. If something critical develops I'll signal for you to call me. Just use that machine of yours to look for me standing outside of your building, I'll be out front waving."
"Good idea. Thanks again, Judy and take care."
He turned off the phone then and faced his friends. "We have a guardian angel in the FBI."
"Every bit of help we can get is appreciated," Leo commented.

Samiha was obviously very worried and moved nervously in her seat next to Luke. "I can't remember when I've ever been more frightened," she said. "I wish, in a way, we'd never found that machine. You were right to call it a Pandora's Box."
Luke placed his hand on her leg in a gesture of comfort and stared with compassion at her.

"I would like to tell you that everything is going to be alright, but I can't," he told her.

"There's nothing I'd rather do than to convince you that there's nothing to worry about, but that would not be very accurate.

"There's nothing we can be sure of. All we can do is go with the flow and hope for the best. Perhaps things *do* happen for a reason, by some unseen design or fate or destiny. I don't know. What I do know, what I am convinced of beyond any doubt, is that how we react to anything affects the outcome. So we have to keep our chins up. We must maintain the best possible attitude and maybe everything will work out alright."

"Well, I may have some good news," Leo interrupted. It was early evening now and he had been working steadily between the computer and the Ocular all day.

"Yeah," Jess agreed, who had stayed with him the entire time, since his return from the Civic Center .

"You might like this interesting bit of snooping," he said as he smiled and patted Leo on his very large back.

"I found something that I think might give us another edge," Leo said as he turned on the massive screen and made a few settings on his keyboard. With his left hand, now deftly familiar with how to operate the Ocular and telescope with one hand, he peered into the eyepiece.

"Watch the screen. What you're going to see next is what appears to be a secret meeting between our Vice President and the top aid to Israel 's Prime Minister.

"This occurred several months ago, when both of these guys were officially somewhere else. The Vice President was presenting an award to a church group in Tulsa who sponsors a program for under privileged housing development. The entire community gets together and builds homes for poor people.

"Our other friend here, was in the States, but according to his itinerary, he was making the rounds at a Jewish health care center for the elderly in North Hollywood ."

Leo looked up at the screen as a new image opened up into clear focus, then he went on,

"All I can say is, wherever they really are, it's no building site for the poor and certainly no health clinic."

Leo clicked a button on his keyboard several times, and for every tap the image loomed closer and closer into full close-up view until an outdoor cafe appeared. Sitting in a pair of plastic chairs next to one of several clean round white tables, talking in deep earnest, were the pair of political dignitaries.

Leo zoomed in on their faces, whose expressions were intently serious and concentrated in grave conversation.

"I'd love to know what they're talking about," Luke commented. Leo looked over at his friend and smiled. "Before the night's out we will. One of my students who doesn't live far from here, is severely handicapped with a hearing disorder but she's a master at reading lips! I emailed her this morning when I figured there might be an occasion to be needing her services. She'd be very happy to help."

Luke studied the area of coffee shop where the two talked together. In clear sight was an adjacent parking lot where several dark colored cars were parked surrounded by two teams of casually attired bodyguards.

A newspaper box near the end of walkway, in front of the small shop displayed today's copy of the Quartzsite Arizona Times. No one else was nearby and except for the obvious, the area appeared to be very deserted.

"Where is Quartzsite?" Jess asked.

"About a hundred miles west of Phoenix , out in the middle of the desert," Leo told him. "It's a very small town mostly filled with retirees, snowbirds and cheap trailer parks. There's less than two thousand residents in the entire town and from the looks of things, most of them are probably still in bed.

"A perfect place where even Elvis wouldn't be recognized."
Leo continued to view and record the meeting for some time, and until the two politicians finally ended their talk, shook hands and rose to leave. After they had disappeared into their vehicles, Leo zoomed in for a close up of their license plates, then he

panned the entire surrounding area, absorbing images of a few lone pedestrians as they made their ways to wherever they were going. He scanned neighboring businesses and shops, and recorded a large marquee at the top of a local bank, that displayed the time, date and current temperature.

Then he took one more shot of the short parade of dark cars as they left the area and headed east on highway US 10.

"I've established the exact time line, so there's no mistaking or disputing when this meeting took place," Leo announced as he pressed the eject button near his CD burner, then slid the disc into a protective envelope and started for the door. "I'll be right back," he told them. "This shouldn't take very long."

When he returned, less than an hour later, his face was flushed white and his expression worried and ill. He looked like he'd seen a ghost.
Samiha rushed to his aid as he slumped into his favorite love seat and passed several pages of hand written notes he'd scribbled to Luke. Samiha tried to comfort him with soothing hands on his shoulders.

"What is it, my friend? What have you learned?" she asked him. Jess leaned next to Luke and together they read the pages of conversation script that Leo had transcribed with the help of his lip reader. Leo let out a long depressing sigh.
"This whole thing is becoming more and more terrible as time goes by," he muttered.
"It appears," he went on, "that what they were talking about was a plan to create mass sympathy among the voting public at large, right before the pending election of our current President. Their objective was two fold. One, to anger the American people so much that the majority of them would support his decision to use military action against Libya; and two, to increase the overall acceptance rating of his Administration.

"So what happened, was a secretly conspired plot that used clandestine operatives, both from our side and theirs, to stage an attack on one of our naval bases in the Middle East , and then place the blame on a group affiliated with the Libyan government."

"What?" Jess shouted. "You've got to be joking!"

Luke was equally astonished. "I remember that attack," he said. "Dozens of young sailors were brutally killed when a truck filled with explosives slammed into their barracks."

Leo rested his head in his hands and stared aimlessly at the floor. "It was all bullshit," Leo mumbled. "The media told us that it had been an attack planned and carried out by terrorists and that certain radical groups had publicly claimed responsibility. None of it was true. Those boys were killed by our own hands and the hands of our allies."

"Those sons of bitches!" Jess repeated several times as he paced the floor and shook his head in disbelief.

"So this meeting that we just witnessed," Leo continued, "was the final collaboration of all of the details leading up to and outlining the time the attack was to occur. I checked. Their schedule was dead on. These two guys were the contacts between both authorities."

Samiha was covering her mouth with her hands in astonishment, and everyone became silent for a while. Then Luke took a couple of deep breaths and looked around the room at each of his friends.

"And we have it all recorded!" he exclaimed and went on. "So you know what we're going to do? We're gonna shove it right down their throats!" He turned to Leo and pointed over at the computer station. "Get to work right now and start making some copies, at least four, of everything derogatory we have on them, including when they followed us from the airport and the shooting. Get copies of the assassination of that King, the meetings with their ambassadors and this grand finale with our two heroes."

To Jess he said,

"You'll return to the Civic Center and drop one of the copies off
to this Bernstien guy, right on his desk!
"I'm gonna call our friend Judy at the FBI and arrange to drop off
a copy with her too."
Leo raised his arm in protest.
"Luke, we need to think this out a bit. None of what we've
learned yet will help to protect you, us or the Ocular."
"No!" Luke demanded. "This ends now!"

Chapter Twenty Four

When Luke called Judy he directed her to a telephone booth on a relatively busy street, miles from Leo's house, where he and Judy watched from vantage spot not far away, parked in Leo's conversion van. As Luke had instructed, Judy was quick to respond and wasted no time hurrying to the booth and retrieved the package Luke had hidden neatly under several telephone books.

It was decided not to meet with Judy in person, to prevent her bosses from asking too many questions or putting Judy in the position that would have required her to detain them.
Luke and Samiha watched her as she inspected the package briefly, then hurried back to her car to head back to her home. Her partner was waiting for her at the entrance and greeted her when she arrived.

"I got here as fast as I could," he told her.
"Perfect timing," she replied as she led him into her apartment, opening the large brown envelope as she moved. Inside, she spilled the contents of the package onto her kitchen counter and found two CD discs and several sheets of paper, filled with typed information.
The first of the sheets was addressed to her. She read it aloud for Michael.

'Dear Judy,
'Once you view the discs you'll understand why I am asking you to help us deliver the enclosed message to whomever it concerns. We were able to produce these recordings with the successful application of the Time Ocular, the machine Samiha's crew discovered along with other investigative tools that friends provided.
'Along with the visual record, I've also included a text transcript of a secret conversation that goes with one of the discs. It

describes in detail, a matter you'll find very interesting, and with all you'll learn with the information here, you'll understand why it is vitally important that these materials get into the right hands.

'The following, are instructions I've set down that must be followed to the letter, without deviation. If they are not, I will not hesitate to deliver this entire package to sources that will investigate all of these matters to the fullest.

'To Whom It May Concern:
'A few days ago, one of the archeological teams that work in affiliation with myself and the University at Loyola in Chicago, under the leadership of Ms. Samiha Salaha, uncovered an object while excavating an ancient living quarters. The object we coined Time Ocular, was proven to be of alien origin and had the scientific capability of being able to *see* into the past.

'It was soon determined that this object was not the only one of its kind, and that years before another identical Time Ocular was discovered and is now in the hands of an allied government, as it has been for some time. It also became apparent that this government has used the machine for their own investigative purposes which largely consisted of the gathering of information that could be used to blackmail others.

'While I would rather not be the cause for the exposing of atrocities committed by influential and high ranking political and judicial people and agencies of the world, *understand that I will do exactly that*, if this alternative is not met with the strictest compliance. Although it may set into motion a tidal wave of ill will and negative reaction by the general public, I will bring to light certain historical events that have been distorted, lied about and covered up for years.

'What I offer is a complete destruction of all of the materials we have compiled and are now in our possession, which include everything contained in this package. All recordings, photographs, and printed evidence will be completely forfeited and never brought to the attention of the general public. We will do this under two conditions.

'The first of these conditions is, that the Time Ocular now in the possession of the allied government, also be destroyed with everything else. We in turn will agree to the simultaneous destruction of our own machine, thereby eliminating any possibility of either side's future use.

'The second condition is that we be left alone from this moment on. That no further reprisals against us or attempts on our lives be pursued.
'The actual disposal of all of these materials will take place on my terms, in a designated area and time of my choosing and under conditions that will not be compromised.
'I'll remind you that the surveillance equipment we can put into action at a moment's notice is quite capable of watching your every move, even as this is being read. Whatever you do, whatever move you make can easily and very quickly be traced and recorded.

'If you choose to comply with these conditions you will instruct your agent, Judy, to signal your intentions by standing out in front of my residence and waving at the sky. We'll be watching.
'We will not wait long for a reply. You have until this morning, 10:30 a.m. If by that time you do not make an attempt to contact us with your unconditional agreement to these conditions, no further contact with us will occur, ever.

'If you agree, we will keep your secrets. It's our desire that the world not know about, or be thrown into utter upheaval over the evils you committed against them. Too many more of the innocent would suffer. Further instructions on the actual location of where we will conduct the destruction of these materials will follow, as soon as your signal to agree is received.'

"It's signed, Luke Ozman," Judy said quietly as she set the papers down and picked up the discs. Then she loaded one of them into her own CD player and watched as the recording played.

The expressions on their faces turned horrific as the pair watched the scenes display of the assassination, the meeting in Quartzite between the two political leaders, and the chase from the airport that ending with Luke's shooting attack. Michael was particularly angered at the events surrounding the naval base plot.

"I can't believe this!" he muttered. "I'm ashamed to be working for these people."

"Just try to remember," Judy cautioned him, "that you work for the American public, and most of them would feel just as you do right now. A few bad apples don't represent all of us, and certainly not the attitude of the people they're supposed to be serving.

"This is some really sick shit," she continued with contempt in her tone. "I never signed on to be a cog in the machinery of lies and murder. But we're gonna have to step lightly now. If asked, we never saw these recordings, and were instructed to deliver them to the bosses unopened.

"We on the same page, Michael?"

Her partner nodded in agreement. "Absolutely."

"Good. Let's wrap these things back up and call in an emergency."

By five o'clock that morning the office of the Chief Supervisor at FBI headquarters was bustling with heated activity. Judy and Michael sat quietly in an adjacent office, and watched through the large glass partition wall as her their boss conferred with his two superiors and the entire four-man guest team of mercenaries. Over and over again, they reviewed the contents of the envelope Judy had delivered. Phone calls were made and received with contentious fever, and shouting among themselves took on an argumentative pitch for over an hour.

Inside the bustling office the leader of the team was furious.

"Never in a million years, did any of us ever imagine the possibility that another time viewing machine existed, let alone that it would fall into the hands of people intelligent enough to know how to use it. Bad luck! This changes everything."
"I told you so," said one of the chief's superiors. "Now we're all up shit's creek."
"When do you expect that spy plane of yours?" the chief interrupted.
"Somewhere around eight. When the pilot gets within range we'll have him land at a designated area of your choice.
"After your call got me out of bed so early this morning I got hold of Burnstien at the Consulate's office. He contacted our people at home and was instructed to have us go along with any decision you deem appropriate.

"Emphasis was leaning toward complying with Ozman's demands. We're on a time clock. This Ozman isn't leaving much room for anything by setting the deadline at 10:30. So for now, you can have your agents go through with the signal he outlined and we'll wait here for further instructions."
"Well, we really have no other choice, do we?" the chief barked. "And frankly, I agree with your people and ours feel the same way. There's too much at stake here. Too many things can go wrong if we try another muscle move. We don't know if these people have spread copies of this stuff all over the halls of every newspaper and TV facility in the country!

"I'm not gonna loose any sleep over the fact that these time viewing machines aren't gonna be around anymore. Up till now they been nothing but a sore on our asses, and now they're right on the verge of taking a big hunk out of yours."

The team leader shrugged his shoulders and looked away from him. "All I can say is that we've been through these compromises before, many times. Both of us. Situations like these keep everything in balance and usually end up for the best. The only thing that worries me is the possibility that these archeologists keep a spare copy of these materials. We cannot allow for that outside chance. We must watch for the moment that this Ozman slips up."

"Slipping up doesn't seem to be in character with this guy," the chief stated, and went on, "but even if he does, I'm gonna gamble that he's the kind of person whose word means something and since you're playing in our back yard right now, we will comply, and nothing else. Those discs have your faces plastered all over them, and we're right in the thick of it with you. The party's over."

The team leader nodded.

"Just let us know where to have the plane land. My men and I will assist, but we'll need help transporting the viewing machine safely to wherever Ozman directs. We'll also need a little time to dismantle the support housing that contains the machine. It was built into a crash-proof pod that won't be easy to open."

"You'll have what you need," the chief acknowledged as he moved to the door that separated Judy and her partner from the main office.

He motioned them to get up as he ordered, "Get over to Ozman's building and get prepared to give him a signal. He instructed us to have you wave toward the sky and indicated that he'd know when it happened."

As soon as the two left, he returned to his desk and began ripping up the pages of the notes Luke had delivered. Then he deposited the torn scraps in a large glass candy tray and set them afire. "We may as well start cleaning this mess up right here."

The leader of the mercenary team paced the floor of their motel room looking very angered and determined. His three associates just sat quietly, watching him seethe with mild rage while they said nothing.

"If these people think that I'm just going to sit back and let them go along with allowing those school teachers to dictate how this operation will go, they're dead wrong! I'll be damned if I'll let them get away with these machines." He blurted in his unique tone of broken English.

"Right now these two machines are in the hands of the wrong people. Our own government for one, and this tribe of grave diggers that have absolutely no idea what they possess, or what to do with it.

"Listen up, guys. Think about this for a minute.

"What if *we* had their machine all to ourselves? Do you have any idea what we could accomplish? We could call our own shots, make our own deals. Hell, we'd be in a power position most only dream about."

"What are you suggesting?" One of his men asked. "That we steal their machine and keep it a secret from our superiors?"

"Why not?" the leader retorted. "They're giving up on it anyway! They're throwing it away...wasting that valuable machine for the sake of politics. And why not get it for ourselves? Who's to stop us?"

His associate shook his head in disagreement. He was clearly against the idea.

"We get paid very well to do what we do, and I for one am perfectly content with following instructions. Why rock the boat that keeps us afloat?"

"I agree." One of the other men offered.

"I wouldn't do anything to screw up the deal we have and the good life we enjoy. Back home we have houses, comforts and all of the political clout we'll ever need. We can go anywhere and do anything we like, with no consequences. Why take chances with messing all of that up?"

The third associate remained silent. He was closest in friendship with the leader and usually leaned toward his viewpoint over any other.

"You guys are having a little problem with seeing the forest for the trees," the leader rambled on.

"With a machine like one of those, that can do the things they say it can, we could have all of those benefits anyway and a lot more! House, comforts and clout? These are table scraps compared to what we could really enjoy!

"Right now we are sitting between two stools occupied by authorities that would stab each other in the back at the drop of a hat. There's no real loyalty between them. Each has something the other either wants or needs and both of them would stoop to any degree to maintain their mutual arrangements. And where are we, *we four*, in this scenario? I'll tell you where! We're the hired help. We're the ones who they rely on to sanitize the messes they make. We clean their dirty laundry and sweep up their garbage!" His tone became more and more aggressive as he continued.

"Listen to me! We've been placed into a situation that can be very, very beneficial to all of us. This is a golden opportunity to take full advantage of yet another one of their messes and come away from this thing as the winners. We're being handed this on a silver platter."

The first of his team who objected to the idea rose to his feet and walked toward the door.

"I don't want anything to do with it," he announced. "My job here is done. You do whatever you want. I'm going out for a beer."

The other partner who was also opposed to the plan got up from his chair and followed him to the door.

"I'll go with you," he said.

After they were gone the leader shook his head in disgust. He looked over at the remaining member of his crew and addressed him by name.

"And what about you, Zeek?

His friend leaned back in his chair and folded his arms before replying. His were cold dead eyes of the kind one could easily associate with a killer shark. He rarely spoke, even in the company of friends, and his allegiance was always on the side of the team leader.

"I go with you, whatever you say."

"Good. These idiots are going to deliver our government's machine into the hands of the scientists. Their plan is to allow Mr. Ozman to go ahead with the destruction of both of them, but we're not going to let that happen. You and I will be waiting for them."

&

Chapter Twenty Five

Leo had the telescope focused in on the entrance of Luke's
building when he and Samiha returned. Jess was sealing up the
final package of photos, discs and notes that was planned to be
delivered Burnstien at the Civic Center as the culminating gesture
of deal, should everything go as planned.

He separated all of the special recordings Leo had produced of
the young Martian as he strolled along the perimeter of the
ancient building site and then later, when he sat near his tent.
These would not be included in the materials given to the
authorities.

Luke and Samiha relaxed with coffee as they and their two
friends watched the large screen with mounting anticipation, the
early morning sights of Lincoln Park West and the area in front
of his building. They did not have to wait very long.

"Heads up, people!" Leo announced excitedly at the appearance
of a familiar car as it pulled in front of the building and stopped.
Judy emerged and anxiously looked up at the sky then waved her
right arm high over her head.
She lowered her arm after a few seconds, walked closer to the
front entrances then looked up again, and once more waved, this
time a little longer.
 "They've agreed to the exchange!" Samiha exclaimed gleefully.
"Oh my God! That's wonderful!"
Luke was smiling widely while Jess and Leo also displayed
expressions of mild satisfaction.

"This is great!" Luke said, and went on, "But it's far from over
yet. We still have to hope that the next few steps of the plan are
followed to the letter. Don't assume for a minute that these guys
are just gonna do everything we demanded of them without some

kind of reservation. They'll be watching for the first opportunity to take advantage of even the smallest mistake I make."

He unfolded some notes that had been tucked away in one of his pockets.
"Hand me the phone," he told Samiha.
He dialed Judy's number and they all watched the screen as she immediately reacted, answering her cell phone.

"Hello Judy. I see that they've agreed to my terms."
"Yes, Luke! I've been with them since before the chickens got up this morning. You really got them frazzled. Our side agreed right away and their people also decided that is was the only intelligent thing to do. Trust me buddy, it seems like things are gonna go your way."
"Go back to your car so you can write," Luke instructed her. "Let me know when you're ready to take down a few notes."
Judy complied, getting quickly back into her vehicle. She held her phone close to Michael's ear and motioned for him to have a pen and note pad ready.
"Go ahead, Luke."
"OK, here's the deal," Luke began.
"There's a steel mill on the south side of the city very near to 127th street and Torrence avenue . The company is called Illinois-Indiana Iron Works and the sign is plain as day, plastered all over the building. The faculty and students have been there several times on physics related projects, so we know it well and we won't be disturbed.
"Only you and one other agent come. In fact emphasize to them that I specifically directed that it be you and only you who handles their Time Ocular, and insist that I demanded there not be an entire cavalry of agents around. I don't want to alarm anyone in the area with too much activity.

"I'll be there alone, with our Time Ocular at the rear of the complex in an area of their main boiler rooms. Just follow the loud sounds and strong smell. You can't miss it.

"You won't see me until I see you. Once that happens, we'll exchange Oculars and I'll walk outside briefly, to test it and make sure they haven't substituted it with a dummy duplicate copy. That shouldn't take me more than a minute or so. When I return, you'll follow me to the actual area were together, we'll dump both machines simultaneously, destroying them in a way I'll show you when we meet up. Once that's done, you and whomever you're with will leave. I remain for a minute or two to give the destruction process enough time to complete and make sure it isn't interrupted or accidentally disturbed by anything or anyone.

"Then I'll leave, and once I'm satisfied, I'll place a call to one of my associates who will drop off the last package of discs and photos to their advisor to the ambassador at the Civic Center. When that's done, there will be no need to bother us ever again. "They don't have to worry. I'll keep my end of the agreement but I have to warn you Judy, every moment will be closely monitored by my associates. Let your bosses know, in no uncertain terms, that if one iota does not go as planned, if they try a single trick, or deviate from this plan in any way, my friends have been instructed to forget about me entirely and go straight to the media. It'll be on the noon news. Do you understand?"
"Yes, Luke," she replied. "Trust me. I'll see this thing through for you and do everything I can to make sure that all goes as smoothly as possible.

"I gotta tell you, though," she continued, "it's a damn shame you have to lose such a magnificent discovery. I'm sure you and friends can't be very happy about that part of it."
"You're right about that Judy. But as I said in my notes to your superiors, I choose the lesser of the two evils, and the well being of my friends and myself over the things that could occur if we didn't do it this way.
"Yeah, it'll be a significant loss that would've have had a profound benefit for mankind as a whole, but I'm convinced that as long as we remain a society infected with the negative impulse

to control others, to justify murder and lies, then the existence of the Ocular is just too big a safety risk to keep around."

"I understand," she answered him. "But personally, just between you and me, I wish you well and I sincerely hope that some day we might meet on friendlier ground, and under better conditions."

"I'm sure I'd like that too, Judy. We all would. You've turned out to a valuable help to this entire experience and I appreciate you very much.

"Now, listen. Remind them that ten-thirty a.m. is the absolute deadline." He glanced at his watch. "That's a little more than three hours from right now."

"I'll handle it, Luke," she assured him, then they ended their conversation.

The four of them continued to watch the screen as Judy's car came to life and pulled away from the curb. Leo followed their movement with the telescope until he was sure that they were headed back in the direction of their office, then he turned to Luke.

"What will you do now, assuming everything goes as planned and this mess is finally behind us?" he asked.

"I need a vacation!" Luke exclaimed with a healthy laugh.

"What will you do about Joseph, Samiha's project manager and that child who was killed?" Leo went on.

Luke just stared at him for a moment before answering. "Do you mean to ask, what retaliation will I take? Because if that's what you mean, I suppose I'll do nothing."

Leo appeared confused. "But don't you think they deserve some kind of punishment for what they did?"

"Deserve?" Luke echoed. "Yes. Will there be consequences for their actions? Of course. But they've already sealed that fate. *They* put the wheels in motion themselves, that will create the consequences they will pay, whether it's in the next five minutes or their next five lives. The Universe doesn't need me to get involved.

"Listen Leo," Luke continued. "Revenge is great stuff for action films, but in the soul it doesn't exist. Reaping what you sow and what goes around come around aren't just witty slogans without basis or meaning. And if I took revenge, if I struck out in anger or for that matter any other negative emotion, greed, hate, or jealously then I'd be no different than they, and I would also create circumstances that would immediately set into motion the consequences for my own actions."

He paused for a moment and seemed to be gazing off before adding,

"I think I'd like to take Samiha on a road trip to visit the country. Maybe drive down to southern California and relax by the ocean."

Leo grinned and nodded affectionately.

"Well, you're more than welcome to use my conversion van. It's got all of the comforts of home and handles nicely on long drives."

"Thanks. But first things first. We still have one more major hurdle to jump."

The Chief led five other FBI agents up the rear steps of the motel where the four mercenaries stayed. It was decided that to avoid any risks, they would stay with their guests and keep them under surveillance until after the exchange and destruction of the Oculars were confirmed.

Unannounced, they moved silently down the corridor until they approached the room doors. The four shared adjoining suites, two occupants for each, and as they moved closer the Chief quietly motioned for three of his men to cover the far entrance while he and the rest of his crew stopped at the first.

After the first couple of knocks on the door one of the men inside opened it immediately. With a toothbrush still sticking out of his mouth the mercenary was wide-eyed with surprise, but said nothing. Clad only in shorts he acknowledged the Chief with a weak nod then let them in.

"Good morning!" The Chief greeted. "Is everyone already awake?"

The man nodded again then motioned to the opened adjoining room door. His leader suddenly appeared in the doorway, also dressed only in his underwear and wearing an expression that quickly changed from surprise to indignation.

"What are you guys doing here?"

One of the Chief's men moved into the opposite suite and opened the outer door to admit the other three agents. Then they rounded up the rest of the guests and brought them back to join the others. The Chief smiled sarcastically at the leader.

"We thought you'd like to have some company for breakfast before you all leave for home today."

"Well you thought wrong!" The leader blurted angrily. "Besides, our flight doesn't leave until after noon."

"We know. But the bosses and I were talking and it occurred to us that it might be best if we made perfectly sure that Ozman's rendezvous went on as scheduled. We want it go on as planned, uninterrupted."

The leader looked around at the faces of his companions as if he'd been the victim of betrayal by one of his own. The Chief continued.

"So we'll just all sit here together, maybe have some coffee and kill a few hours. Then we'll leave and you boys can be on your way."

The leader moved over to a chair in the corner of the room and dropped down into the seat.

"Why?" He demanded. "What's going on?"

"Just like I said," the Chief explained, " We're just making sure everything goes smoothly. At this stage of the game we realize that temptations can sometimes overcome reason, and right now we can't take that chance. So just sit back, enjoy the fine company for a short time. We'll be gone soon, then you can go about your business of catching your flight home."

Samiha was an excellent driver and navigated the large conversion van very well as she parked it a quarter of a mile away from the south side steel mill.
She turned to Luke, pulled him close and embraced him for a long time, then kissed him passionately on the lips.
"I wish you weren't the one to have to go through with this part of it," she whispered to him as tears welled up in her eyes.
"I have to," he answered. "I can't expect, nor would I ask, anyone else to do something as critical as this. Don't worry. Everything will be alright. Don't forget, we'll have Judy there and I feel really good about her. I trust that lady now, more than ever."
He stroked her hair, and held her face in his hands, then returned her kiss.
"Everything will be fine," he repeated. "Lock the doors after I'm gone," he instructed her, then picked up the over night bag that contained the Ocular and headed down the street in the direction of the steel mill.

He removed a cell phone from his jacket pocket and dialed Leo's number. "Got me in your sights?" he asked while looking up at the clouds.
"I'm watching your every move," Leo responded.
"OK. Ring twice and hang up if you see anything suspicious, as we planned."

Luke glanced at his watch just before entering the rear doors of the spacious complex of enjoined buildings which made up the vast steel mill facility. It was 10:15 in the morning, and so far everything appeared to be going smoothly. Once inside he donned a yellow hard hat that he found hanging on a rack against the wall, and headed through a maze of football field sized rooms filled with the clanging of metallic machinery and loud shouting from teams of scattered employees.

He then proceeded up a narrow iron staircase that led to a upper level catwalk that lined the entire length of the boiler room area. He then hid himself from view behind a series of vertical pipes and watched the entrance.

Chapter Twenty Six

Promptly, at 10:30, Judy appeared in the doorway, carrying the Ocular in her arms and followed closely by her partner. No one else was present. Luke waited until they had walked almost to the center of the massive room below him, before he called out.
"Up here, Judy!" he shouted, well above the screeching of the machine noise.
He pointed at her partner Michael.
"You stay there. Judy, take the steps up and follow me," he directed.
She complied, and wasting no time, quickly climbed the staircase to his level and moved in behind him. He led her across the entire length of the room which ended at an opening to yet another large area that was filled with the smell of burning metal, and light wisps of white smoke. The concrete floor below them revealed four super sized vats of red hot boiling molten metal, that bubbled noisily and strain the eyes to look at. The heat was intense.

Luke stopped on the catwalk near one of the many spaced escape exits that dotted the catwalk and served as easy access ways to the cool air outside. He waited until she had caught up to him, then greeted her with a smile.

"Nice to see you in person again."
"It's nice to see you too, Luke, though I can think of a million other nicer places to meet rather than here."
Luke chuckled. "Is everything going to go as planned, Judy?"
"It appears that way, Luke," she answered him as they exchanged Oculars.
"Good. Wait here a second," he told her. "I'm gonna step outside for a moment and make sure this thing is the real McCoy."
He disappeared through the escape door that opened up onto an outdoor balcony directly overlooking a rear parking lot.
He removed the cell phone from his pocket again and dialed Leo.

"Do you see me?"

"I got you, Luke," Leo responded.

Luke put the phone away and pulled out the Ocular needle from his shirt pocket, then raised the machine to eye level. In seconds he was satisfied. The low pitched hum that always accompanied the start-up sounds when the Ocular warmed up was clear and familiar. He was impressed with the exactness of the form of the machine. It was, in every detail, a perfect duplicate of his own Ocular. He looked up at the surrounding area and raised the machine to his eyes while he touched the base with the needle. It worked. He gave the thumbs up sign to the sky then rejoined Judy back inside. He motioned for her to follow until they were positioned directly over one of the boiling vats of liquid metal. Judy winced at the increased heat, but stayed with him.

"I'm half tempted to let you leave with both of these things," she shouted to him.

"That would never work," he replied. "Besides, a deal is a deal." He took one look at the vat below then threw the Ocular into the fiery liquid. They watched the splash it created and listened to the whooshing sound it made as it kicked up a small cloud of white smoke before it sank.

Judy hesitated for a moment, looked into Luke's eyes, then dropped the Ocular over the rail and into the molten metal. Together they stared at the wake of the final destruction of the greatest discoveries in all of archeological history. Luke was deeply moved and sadness lined his eyes as he shook his head. Judy reached over to him, and touched his shoulder.

"I'm sorry Luke. I'm sorry you had to do it this way."

He said nothing as he continued to observe the trails of smoke that rose from the burning pit for a few more minutes before even they dissipated in the air. The sounds each machine made as they melted and sank had ended, and now there was no trace.

"I'm gonna leave now, Luke. I was told to report in as soon as it was done." Luke turned to her and extended his hand. They shook hands warmly and Judy smiled at him.

"You take care of yourself," she said, then walked back to join her partner. He watched her leave then looked back down at the

boiling metal once more, lingering for a few minutes and thinking about what could have been. Then he took a few deep breaths and started back to Samiha and the waiting van.
Samiha could sense his emotion immediately.

"Did something go wrong? What's the matter?" she asked him.
"No. Everything went according to the way we supposed it would."
Samiha was sympathetic and stroked his cheek but said nothing as she started the van up and pulled away.
Luke dialed Leo one more time.
"Signal Jess to drop the final package off at Burnstiens office. We'll be home soon."

Jess had already returned from his final trip to the Civic Center , delivering the envelope of information without incident. He and Leo were busily reviewing the recordings made earlier of the young Martian as he sat outside his tent and went through a pantomime of strange hand movements while displaying his large world map. Luke and Samiha finally returned from the south side and joined them in the observation room. Leo was scribbling notes on a pad at his computer station while Jess made measurements on world map of their own that they had set up on an easel next to them. They stopped what they were doing when Luke and Samiha entered the room.

Leo rose to greet his friends.
"No one followed you as far as I could tell," Leo began. "I scoured the entire neighborhood around where you parked and followed your movements for a while after you left the steel mill, but saw nothing that would indicate that they were around. Looks like we did it."
"I suppose that's a good thing," Luke murmured, as he slumped in a chair disgustedly, still moody over the loss of the machine.

"That guy Burnstien was on the phone when I walked into his office," Jess reported. "When I threw the package on his desk, he dropped the phone and snatched it up like a hungry rat, then ran out of the room without a word."
Luke nodded in acknowledgement but remained silent.

Leo moved closer to his friend and bent down to gently grasp both of his shoulders as he gave him one of his beaming smiles. "Luke, I found something very interesting. This is gonna make your day!" He was very excited and went on. "If I'm right about this, you're gonna be dancing with joy in a few minutes."
"What is it?" Luke asked him.
Leo motioned for him to watch the screen and returned to his desk. He pointed to the large world map that he a Jess had set up on the easel, then rewound the recording until the screen displayed an image of the young Martian, seated on the ground next to his tent.

"I've been a little confused over this scene since the first time I saw him making these strange movements and pointing to the various marked spots on his map," Leo explained. "So I took my time and studied it again, and Jess saw something that shed a new light on the whole picture."
"The movements he's making aren't strange at all," Jess offered. "Not if you look closely at them. He's doing the same thing you and Leo did every time you two guys operated the Ocular."
Leo zoomed in the view until he had enlarged the young man's image as he pointed to the first spot on his map.
"I've calculated the exact coordinates of that X he's marked," Leo continued, "and it's precisely where Samiha's crew found the ocular. There's no mistaking it."
"Really?" Samiha questioned.
"Yes. And this second one a little to the south, happens to be right near a town called Qoseir, where the Sodmein Cave is and where they reportedly found the first Ocular."
Luke's interest was at its peak now as he listened to Leo and moved closer to the map they'd set up on the easel. He pointed to

X marks in both, the South American location and the one in
Arizona .
"And what of these?" he asked Leo.
"The one in Peru is an area known as Macchu Picchu and has
been described as the most peaceful place on Earth. Like Giza ,
half way around the world, Macchu Picchu is an ancient village
built thousands of years ago by residents who were able to
transport giant perfectly cut stones that weigh well into the tons,
and construct a series of mysterious temples and pyramids that
defy explanation.

"The village is set high into the mountains, at treacherous
heights, where they carved terraces for farming and chose to
build a home well above rich valleys that easily could've
provided them every resource they would need to get along.
"Their temples and pyramids have stairs that lead to nowhere,
and the shapes of the cut stones are so precise that they would
marvel laser technology. Macchu Picchu, like Giza is believed to
be one of the most powerful sources for vortex energy that attract
spiritualists from all over the world. This energy is mystical, and
is described as focal power spots. UFO buffs love it too, and visit
the area to see ancient carvings on walls of flying craft.

"If I were the one selected to find a place suitable for hiding one
of the Oculars, I'd pick Macchu Picchu too.
"The location indicated in Arizona is just as interesting. In fact, I
double checked it time and time again just to be positive about
what I learned about it.
"You see, the careful way they were all marked on our friends
map are very indicative of exact locations and when I cross
referenced the known longitudes and latitudes of the first two, it
was easier to verify the one in Arizona .

"I gotta tell you, it took me by surprise, because it turns out that
the mark points to a little resort town now known as Sedona. It's
about thirty miles south of Flagstaff and near the edge of where
the Grand Canyon begins. The most interesting thing about that

location is the fact that the X falls smack dab in the center of Bell Rock!"

"What's Bell Rock?" Samiha asked him.

"It's a very old, weather beaten piece of mountain, that some say might have once been a pyramid, but now after thousands of years of corrosion, has taken the shape of a bell."

"Wow," Luke muttered

. "Do you think that our friend from Mars was trying to tell us where other Oculars were buried?"

Leo grinned widely.

"He couldn't have been more explicit if he'd sent us a memo!" Leo proclaimed excitedly. "And I'll show you what confirms it without a doubt.

"I'm gonna run the recorded sequence of him making all of those strange hand gestures and movements he was going through, so watch closely."

Leo rewound the recording once again, taking it back to the moment the young man brought his map out from the tent and unfolded onto the ground and began to point at the various vocations.

"Watch his hands," Leo directed.

"See how he appears to be holding both hands up in front of his face, in a posture that looks like he's in prayer?"

"Yes," Luke acknowledged.

"Well, he's not praying at all. He's going through the motions of holding an Ocular up to his line of sight, and panning the surrounding area!"

"He sure is!" Samiha exclaimed.

"You are right. That's just what he's doing!"

Luke was ecstatic.

"Now watch what he does next," Leo continued. "He points at the four locations, clearly marked on his map, then raises his hands up once again, in the same movements, just like you've done dozens of times while holding the Ocular yourself.

"It's as if he's telling us that other Oculars have been left in other locations, when he points to the Sedmein Cave, the Peru spot and the one in Arizona!"

"It couldn't be more plainly described," Jess offered.

"I just wonder if there is a chance that the machines are still there."

"Well," Luke began, with brand new hope and conviction in his tone,

"I can't think of anything more deserving or worth looking into. I want to visit this place Sedona and find out. And if it's not there, go on to Peru if need be and look there too!"

"I've been to Sedona," Leo stated.

"There's a good chance it hasn't been disturbed for several good reasons, number one, although it's a popular landmark attraction that draws thousands of sight seekers and photographers every month, it's not readily accessible to the general public."

"Why?" Luke asked him.

"Because it's off the beaten path of the road that leads from the main highway and the town of Sedona itself, and barred from walking near it by fences and warning signs all along that road.

"It's probably no more than a few hundred yards off the road, and clearly visible, but no one walks near it without risk of arrest by the local authorities, for safety."

"But it is accessible, I mean one could approach it, unseen maybe?" Luke inquired.

"Sure it could be done," Leo assured him.

"A couple of people could slip through the fence at a point down the road and maybe make their way in the dark around to the rear of it without being seen.

"But then you'd have to climb it, and there's the snakes to worry about, because that's when they come out, at night."

"Would you like to see Bell Rock right now in living color?" Leo asked them.

"I'd love nothing better!" Samiha replied, smiling.

Luke nodded and Leo went to work right away, calibrating adjustments on his computer to align the telescope to the proper coordinates. Then he inserted a blank CD disc into his burner. "I'll record what we look at now and later, when you're there, you can refer to it by using the CD recording in the unit I have in the conversion van."

"Good idea," Luke offered.

In a few minutes, Leo was ready and the screen suddenly came to life showing an overhead view of the rocky mountainous region over Sedona.

He watched the screen closely as he began to zoom in nearer and nearer, as he clicked a button on his keyboard several times. With each click, the image enlarged and the resolution became clearer until finally, he reached a viewing distance that simulated a few hundred feet in the air. "There it is!" he announced.

What they saw was one of the most breathtaking and colorful locations in the western United States . Just south of the Grand Canyon , the low mountains were a splendid blend of orange, reds and browns, unlike anything normally associated with desert terrain.

Immense gorges and jutting rocks in an array of magnificent shapes and sizes blanketed the entire area.

"It's stunningly beautiful!" Samiha exclaimed.

"Any artist's dream come true," Luke agreed.

Leo pointed to a specific spot on the screen and clicked a button on his keyboard several more times, and soon they all understood the reason for the name, Bell Rock.

"Wow," Jess uttered in amazement.

"That is truly some-thing to behold!"

Leo zoomed in slightly closer and stopped when he was able to focus in on the top of the massive rock, whose peak had long ago been smoothed to a plateau roundness by thousands of years of winds and weather.

"Climbing it should not present much of a problem with all of the layered crevices and foot holds," Leo suggested.

"I've climbed lots worse," Samiha stated.

"And higher and steeper too!"

"I have too," Luke offered.

"That doesn't look very difficult at all. With the right tools and equipment, it doesn't appear too bad."

Leo continued to pan over the top of Bell Rock, zooming in to only a few feet above it. The surface was pock marked with dozens of narrow caves and cracks that could easily allow access to a number of different entry points, and most likely served as a haven for some of the local wildlife.

"It won't be easy to search. You'd have to get very lucky to find the right passageway if the weather and time hasn't played tricks with it."

"The prize will be well worth the effort," Luke proclaimed.

"Besides, what better way to spend a vacation than mixing a little exploration with relaxing in such a lovely location?"

He turned to Samiha and asked,

 "What do you think?"

"Let's go!" she exclaimed without hesitation.

"**W**hy in the world would you want to quit now?" Michael asked Judy, his expression one of total disbelief.

"You'll be up for a pay increase and promotion by the end of this month, and you have eight years of your life invested in Federal service. Besides that, agents with your qualifications are few and far between. Why would you even consider throwing all that away?"

"I've made up my mind," Judy told him, as they sat across from one another in a booth at a small corner restaurant near her home. "It's very difficult for me to wake up every morning knowing I have to go to work for people who have allowed the kind of lies, public deceit, and murder to go on unchecked and even orchestrated by themselves for their own self-centered interests. This is supposed to be a democracy, instead what we've witnessed in just the past few days borders on the fence of raw dictatorship."

Michael dropped his eyes down and stared at the coffee in his cup. He was clearly upset.

"I could never get lucky enough to land another partner like you, Judy."

She reached across the table and gently patted one of his hands with one of her own.

"You have a good, kind heart Michael. I've liked you since day one and I'll always be your friend. This doesn't mean that I'm quitting you. But try to understand why I choose to do this.

"You're married with a young family to think about, while I'm all by myself. And I don't have to live with this kind of corruption. I've seen what it's done to some of the agents I've worked with during most of the past decade, who begin their careers with the FBI with high aspirations of making a difference with genuine contribution, only to wind up taking a back seat to their initial convictions because of a paycheck.

"I don't need to buckle under or close my eyes to the activities I feel should not go on among people in our ranks. The citizens of this country and the world need to trust us again. They need folks in positions like ours that they can rely on for truth and protection. How can they have that, when our own superiors are rotten and without morals?

"It appalls me to no end, at the knowledge that even one among us has compromised that kind of trust."

Michael interrupted her with a raised hand.

"Don't you think that there might be an opportunity for you to stay within the system and try to make changes in those ills from within?"

"I thought about that, Michael. But No I do not. I'm completely convinced that I'd never be in a position to change anything. The corruption reaches too high up the ladder of administration and even if I were to remain for years to come, I'd never be allowed in the inner circles of authority that would permit my input on anything.

"And right now, they represent the broadest definition of everything I am ethically against, everything I came to work for the FBI in the first place."

"So what will you do?" Michael asked her.

She just shrugged her shoulders.

"I'm not hurting for money, so it's not like I'll have to jump right into another job right this minute. I don't know yet, Michael. Frankly I never really had a desire to do anything other than law enforcement, so maybe eventually I could land something on a small town police force, or something along those lines. But for right now I think that I'll just take my time about it. I need to clear my head and maybe take an extended vacation."

"What will you tell the chief?"

"You mean, what excuse am I going to give him for my decision to leave?"

Michael nodded.

"Well I won't go into a lot of detail. I won't let on that I know more than he thinks I know, but I will tell him my feelings on these mercenary characters they do business with. I'll let him know, without pulling any punches, that I don't agree with their collaboration with thugs.

"So when is all of this going to happen?" he asked.

"Right away! I don't want to remain another minute, Michael. I planned to stop by the office today and turn everything in, that's why I had you meet me here this morning."

"Thanks for thinking of me first," he told her.

"Whatever you do, I'm sure it'll be the right decision and I'll always miss you."

Judy rose then and leaned to kiss him on his cheek.

"I'll miss you too. But you don't have to be a stranger. You know where I live. Call me anytime."

Then she left.

Chapter Twenty Seven

"These switches on the overhead console control the circuits that direct the power to the interior lights, the TV and VCR/CD unit and the remote satellite internet connection service," Leo explained, as he instructed Luke and Samiha on the operation of some of the gadgets in his conversion van.

"There's even a small portable gas operated generator in the cabinet under the sink, should you even need to use it."

"Yeah, all that's fine, but where's the swimming pool?" Luke joked.

Samiha was very impressed.

"This is really something else! What a vehicle! You're so generous to let us use it, Leo."

"Think nothing of it," Leo remarked.

"Most of the time it just sits in the garage unused; besides, I can't think of a better cause."

Earlier Luke had decided that is was still too soon to return to his apartment, just to retrieve a few items of clothing and shaving supplies.

"We'll just buy what we need on the way," he decided.

"No sense taking a chance that my place is still being watched."

"Credit cards leave a paper trail," Leo told him, as he handed Luke a thick envelope packed with cash.

"Jesus!" Luke reacted.

"There's three inches of money in here!"

"Ten grand," Leo confirmed." A little walking-around cash. You can pay me back when you return with another Ocular."

Luke acknowledged his friend's kindness with a grin and a nod.

"You can bet I will. Thank you."

Jess helped Leo pack their cooler with soft drinks and sandwiches and when everything was ready, they bid their farewells in the driveway.

"I'll peek in on you from time to time with the telescope," Leo offered.

"Stay in touch often with your cell phone, and use the on board
internet service if you need it."
Samiha hugged Jess and then Leo.
"I'll miss you both, very much. Please take care," She told them,
then climbed into the passengers side of the van.
Luke stopped for a final word with his two friends. "You guys
keep your guard up and your eyes open. We may well be out of
the woods now, but it won't hurt to stay alert. Hopefully, I'll
return real soon and we'll get back to the business of getting on
with our lives and enjoying the new things we can learn with the
Ocular."
He shook their hands warmly, then waved good-by to them as he
mounted the drivers seat of the van.

He took a westward route along Interstate Eighty, that would cut
through Iowa , Nebraska then Colorado and finally the northern
tip of Arizona , and Flagstaff where they'd head south to Sedona.
It was perfect weather for the thirty-hour drive and Luke was in
good spirits as he settled into the comfortable cockpit and
enjoyed the idea of looking forward to the trip.

In slightly more than two hours, they had reached the Quad Cities
and crossed one of the long bridges that spanned the great
Mississippi River, into Iowa .
"I'm gonna pull over into this gas station coming up on the right
and top off the tank," Luke announced. "So take a minute and
stretch your legs, or use the bathroom if you want."
Samiha left the van and walked over to the station's convenient
store while Luke undertook the task of fueling up the van. She
returned shortly carrying two steaming cups of coffee while she
strolled nonchalantly and beamed a smile that lit up her face from
ear to ear.

Luke could not help but to grin back at her.
 "What did you run into that's got you so giddy?"

She kissed him lightly on the cheek, handed him one of the coffees and said,
"You!" I'm just feeling so relieved that we're away from all of that drama and especially happy that I'm with you on this wonderful trip."
"Boy are you easy," he kidded her, and went on,
"I'm glad too. I suppose we do have plenty to be grateful for, especially our buddy from the FBI, Judy. It sure felt good to have her on our side."
"I agree," Samiha commented.
"I'd like to give her a call and thank her. I never got a chance to before we left."
"That's not a bad idea," Luke said.
"Go ahead and call her.
"I'm sure she'd be pleased to hear from you, and I'd like to say hello myself."

Luke paid for the gas then returned and opened the sliding door on the side of the van and sat in one of the comfortable captains chairs, and dialed Judy's cell phone number. He handed the phone to Samiha, and sipped his coffee as he watched her.
"Hi Judy!" she greeted the other almost immediately. "This is Samiha, Luke's friend."

She listened to the other end of the line for a few minutes, and smiled widely before continuing.
"It's nice to hear your voice too. I just wanted to tell you how much your help has meant to me, and to thank you, ever so much for everything. Yes... he's right beside me." She handed the phone back to Luke.
"Hello Judy!" Luke greeted her warmly then listen quietly as she spoke to him for several minutes. Luke's expression showed concern, and he looked up at Samiha when he said, "You quit the FBI?" Samiha listened more intently with a puzzled look on her face.

Luke continued to listen for several more minutes, then let out a sigh of resignation and said,

"Well, in a way I'm disappointed to hear about it. I'm sure that you enjoyed your profession and it had to be a major decision for you.

"I know of several people, including myself, that will remain in your debt for a very long time for the efforts you displayed when helping us.

"I told you before, I had good feelings about you, and the only thing I can tell you now, is the same thing you offered me on the first day we met. And that is, to feel free to call me anytime. You are definitely a friend."

He listened again as Judy responded, and talked to him for a few more minutes before he responded.

"Listen Judy. I'm gonna give you my friend Leo's phone number and address, where we stayed, hiding while all this went on. I'm positive he'd like to meet you or hear from you. Maybe you could call or stop by and check in on him and our other friend, Jess. They'd be very pleased and although Jess doesn't live there, chances are, after all we've been through together these past few days, he's likely to hang around there a bit more than usual. They're great guys."

Luke relayed the details of Leo's telephone number and home address then went on,

"I'll call him myself from here. We're on the road, heading west on another expedition that I'll instruct him to tell you all about. I won't go into detail on the phone now. You'll understand. Have Leo take you through a guided tour of his famous observation room where we were able to track your movements and where he keeps his massive telescope that we used in our surveillance. I'm sure you'll find it very interesting and I know that you'll enjoy their company."

Luke thanked her again, and promised to stay in touch before turning off the cell phone.

"What a twist of events," he commented to Samiha.

"I would've never guessed that she'd actually be moved to quit her job over this."

Samiha shook her head.

"I'm not totally surprised. After all, she's a genuine person with a kind heart. In the short time we've known her, it's been very easy for me to see that."
Luke nodded in agreement.
"No question about it." And he continued,
"She told me just now that she'd been pretty upset with her boss. On the day that she quit, she let him know how very disappointed and let down she felt over the atmosphere of tolerance that was allowed in dealing with characters she believed they had no business associating with under any circumstances."
They finished their coffee and rested a bit longer, but Luke was anxious to get a lot more ground covered and soon they were back on the highway heading west.

Judy was pleasantly surprised by the phone call. She felt flattered that Luke trusted her by sharing the phone number and address of his friend Leo, where the pair had holed up for most of the week. So when she decided to call Leo that evening she was not disappointed. Luke, as promised, had informed Leo that she'd be getting in touch with him and as it turned out, both Leo and Judy were delighted and looking forward to meeting each other.

When she arrived at his beautiful home the next night she was at first surprised then suddenly alarmed when she approached the front doors to find them slightly ajar. Her instincts and professional training immediately sent up warning flags that were very soon confirmed with the sounds of loud angry shouts that came from deep within the luxurious home.
Although she had turned in her federally issued nine millimeter Glock hand gun days earlier, she was an ardent fan of target shooting and the licensed owner of another that she kept tucked away in her small hand bag.

She removed her shoes at the steps outside and drew the weapon out from its holster, then cautiously entered the foyer.
The sounds were coming from the hall that led to Leo's observation room, and she carefully made her way along the wall until she stopped just short of the hall's entrance. The voices

were very distinct now and she was able to understand every word clearly.

"Look at your friend!" someone demanded.

"I said look at him, you fat son of a bitch!" the voice repeated, this time with more intensity.

"See what happens when you don't answer my questions right away?"

Judy dropped down to one knee and carefully peered around the corner of the wall and into the observation room. She could see Leo sitting on the floor, propped up against a file cabinet. His nose was bleeding profusely and his eyes and cheeks were puffed and swollen from a very recent beating. At his feet, sprawled full length on the floor in front of him, was Jess. Blood still trickled slightly from the stub of his left forefinger that had been severed at the knuckle, and there was a neat hole in his forehead from a point blank gunshot wound.

She immediately recognized the two men who stood over him as part of the team of mercenaries that she'd encountered during the meetings of the previous days. The quiet one was the leader of the crew.

"See fat boy? I told you you'd tell us what we needed to know! And now, get ready to join your friend."

The talker raised his gun and aimed it at Leo's head. At that second Judy fired two quick shots that slammed into the man's back and dropped him like a rock. The other wheeled about in a surprised reaction and got off three shots of his own. They flew harmless past Judy as she ducked and fired again. Careful to avoid Leo, Judy spun flat on the floor and fired once more, but the other man had already darted toward the far end of the room. Covering his head with his folded arms he launched himself through a window that led out to the rear yard. He was instantly back on his feet and Judy could hear him scrambling away through the shrubbery.

Judy moved forward slowly, her weapon leveled at arms length. She paused for a moment to look down at Jess's lifeless body then proceeded to the smashed window and searched the yard but could detect no more movement. The leader of the mercenary team had gotten away.

She returned to Leo who was wide eyed, breathing very heavily and very much in a state of shock.

"Take it easy, buddy. I'm Judy," she comforted him.

"I'm gonna get you some help." She looked around the room, found his phone and dialed up an emergency FBI response number. She barked in a quick code with instructions of her whereabouts, then called the local police using 911. Then she returned to Leo.

He was obviously distraught and emotionally devastated as he mumbled something incoherent under his breath. Judy moved closer to him and gently stroked his head and neck.

"Try to take it easy. It's all over now. You're safe," she consoled him.

"We're gonna get you to a hospital, and get you all fixed up."

"We told them... they know," Leo whispered

"We told them everything..." He repeated with a gut wrenching look of horror and regret.

Judy leaned closer and held his face in both of her hands.

"Told them what? What do they know?"

Leo looked down at Jess's lifeless body and began to sob uncontrollably.

"We told them and they killed him anyway. They cut off his finger and then they shot him."

Tears flowed freely down Leo's cheeks as he continued to weep between gasps of short breaths. Judy hugged him closer to her body and continued to rub his back and neck in an attempt to calm him down.

"Leo, I want you to tell me what they know."

He took several deep breaths and his sobbing started to subside. He looked into Judy's eyes and said,

"We found evidence of two other Oculars that were purposely buried in separate locations. Luke and Samiha are on their way to Sedona , Arizona to try and find one of them. Jess and I were forced to tell what we knew about where he was."

The blaring sounds of police sirens filled the neighborhood and drew louder as they got closer to Leo's house, while Judy became suddenly aware of the gravity of what Leo had just explained. She thought about it for a moment then told him,

"Say nothing to any of the police who come here about it. Keep it to yourself and when you're asked, just say that they were looking for Luke and you did not know where he was. This is very important Leo. Do you understand me?"

Leo nodded. "I understand."

"I'll stay with you," she went on.

"We'll go to the hospital together then we'll figure this all out, just you and me, and everything will be alright, OK?"

Leo nodded again, as more tears flowed down his bloodied face. Within minutes the house was filled and surrounded by police and FBI agents. An ambulance crew was standing by to await instructions and the first crowd of responding agents burst into the observation room, led by Judy's ex-boss. Michael was right behind him looking very perplexed.

"We got your distress call." The Chief began,

"And at first when we recognized that it was you, we thought it was some kind of mistake. What are you doing here?"

"I was invited," Judy snapped at him.

"I got a call from Luke Ozman last night. And not to change the subject, but I just shot and killed one of your "guests" in there and the one that got away was the leader of your mercenary team friends."

The chief was genuinely surprised.

"What?" They should've been back on their own territory by now! We gave them specific orders to get out of the country immediately and leave things lay as they were."

Judy did not try to hide her anger.

"Well at least two of them didn't listen to you, and now one's dead and the other is on the loose."

"Judy, trust me on this one," the chief explained.

"They were told to get out and to keep away from further involvement with the entire situation.

"Now, come on! We need to get to the bottom of this and focus on what's going on right now."

"You focus. I'm leaving!" she retorted.

"You forget, I don't work for you any more!"

Michael winked at her from behind the chief's back as Judy turned away from him and waved over the ambulance crew.

"We'll need your statement," the chief called after her.

She ignored him, went back to the steps outside and retrieved her shoes and purse, then climbed into the ambulance with Leo.

At the hospital, they spent over two hours in the emergency room. Judy was relieved that all of Leo's injuries proved to be superficial and when she realized that he'd be treated and released she called for a taxi.

હ

"There is a teaching among our Earthly brethren." The elder began, and he continued.

"It's ideology exists in several of their most popular sects. It suggests that they practice the Presence of *Source* in every moment, with every breath and movement. It directs them to have faith in the truth that something powerful and all encompassing holds them up. That even without knowing but in faith they would rest in the conviction that being children of *Source* and not of the world they perceive, their eventual peace is assured."

His younger companion smiled at the other.

"And we will help them along their way when we can." He said.

The elder smiled.

"Yes."

"And they will learn that the way is made clear when it is understood that there is but one Self, even while another is

appearing as you. *I am,* they will come to understand, is that One
Self *even if I* appear as a beggar or thief or enemy. Then will it
become easy to forgive, knowing that One is forgiving oneself.
 "Achieving that union with Sourse does not occur all at once.
For our brethren here on Earth it is a process, and will require
first of the acceptance of the possibility that *Source* actually
exists. They will need to meditate and contemplate this truth until
a firm conviction is developed where there is no doubt that
something maganamous in behind everything that the eyes can
see, their hands can touch and their ears can hear. And that
something is the only power there is.

"As they persist in their realization of *Source* they will need also
to understand that they cannot possibly enter in union with
Source while entertaining any sort of negative beliefs toward life.
They can no longer justify being cruel or condemnation of any
kind. They must surrender their own worldly positions and
opinions, because like their emotions of hate, distain and
vindictiveness they are meerly an egoic smoke screen that hides
all access to who and where they really are."

Back at Leo's house, only two uniformed police officers from the
local department remained, standing idly near their patrol car,
having been instructed to hang around for a few hours longer.
One of them helped Leo out of the taxi when they pulled up,
while Judy stayed back for a moment to speak to the other.

 "Any sign of the one who got away?" she asked him.
 "None. We followed a trail of busted up bushes and flowers all
the way through the neighborhood and one block over, where
they must have had their car parked and hidden. We were kind've
hoping we'd find a trace of blood, thinking that you might've
winged him or something."
 "Well, thanks," Judy offered.

"I'll be staying here with this man tonight, so if you need anything, just ring the doorbell."

The officer shook his head.

"We're out of here by midnight, but thanks anyway."

Judy followed Leo and the other officer into the house and straight to the observation room where Leo stopped and looked at the police outline of Jess's fallen body. There were still blood splatters on the floor and near the file cabinet.

Judy thanked the officer for his help before he left to rejoin his partner outside, then placed her arm around Leo's shoulders.

"There was nothing you could do," she reassured him. "None of this is your fault."

Leo just nodded his head silently, still very upset over the death of his friend.

"Leo, I need you to tell me as much as you can about exactly where Samiha and Luke are headed, and what their plans are.

"This animal who got away has several hours head start and I can guarantee that the very first thing on his mind after he escaped, was to follow your friends. So we need to stop him if we can."

Leo looked up from the floor and into Judy's eyes.

"What could we do?" he asked her.

"We could beat him to it. I could go out there myself, to Arizona , and try to help anyway I can."

"You'd do that?"

She nodded.

"In a heartbeat. So let's get to it. Give me every bit of detail that I can use."

&

"You can take one of two routes to get to Sedona from here," the gas station attendant explained to Luke. They had stopped to rest and fill the tank in Flagstaff early in the morning of the final day of their trip.

"You can get back on the interstate and head south for about a half an hour until you see the sign for the Sedona cut off or if you'd like, take in some really nice scenery by going up here to highway 89a and go down that way. It's a longer ride but I promise you a spectacular view of winding mountain roads and beautiful landscape."

"Let's take the long way!" Samiha urged excitedly.

Luke smiled at her and thanked the attendant for his help.

"OK. We'll take the scenic route," he announced.

They slept the night before in the van at a rest area along the highway, just east of Flagstaff and now they were only a few short miles from their destination. At the rest area they were able to clean up and change clothes but Luke could tell that Samiha was anxious to settle into a motel.

After a couple of cups of gas station coffee they headed back out in the direction of highway 89a and the route that would take them down the steep mountain and into Sedona.

The attendant's advise proved to be very worthwhile. The view was breathtaking as it twisted and turned past sheer cliffs and gorges, at times slowing to a crawl at sharp corners or steep inclines. Samiha's eyes were wide with awe as their vehicle moved from one splendid view to another with every mile.

Luke's cell phone rang about half way down the mountain and he pulled over into an over lookers observation area before answering it.

"Hello Leo!" Luke greeted his friend, then listened intently, without speaking for several long minutes. Samiha watched him nervously as his expression took on severe lines of concern and worry. He closed his eyes and rubbed his forehead.

"Is there something wrong?" she asked him, cautiously.

Luke didn't even hear her question as he continued to hold the telephone to his ear and listened.

After what seemed like a very long time he took a deep breath and finally spoke.

"Ok Leo. We'll be careful. Thank you."

"What is it?" Samiha insisted.

Luke turned to her and took her hands into his own.

"Jess has been killed."

"What?" she screamed as her eyes began to well up in tears.
"It happened late last night," Luke explained.

"Two of our mercenary thugs visited Leo's house and forced Jess and he to tell them where you and I are. Judy happened upon them just in time to save Leo, but Jess had already been shot." Luke avoided going into specific detail about how Jess's finger had been cut off or of how both of them, as Leo explained, had been subjected to torturous beatings.

Samiha was crying openly now and Luke held her close to his chest.

"My God!" she wailed.

"When is this ever going to end?"

Luke was equally distraught but held his emotions in check as he continued to try to comfort her.

"Leo told me that we had to move quickly if we were going to have any success with finding the other Ocular. Judy is on her way even as we speak and will call us as soon as she gets to town. They believe that the leader of the gang, who escaped last night, may also be on his way here. It stands to reason because he knows what we're looking for."

"Oh no!" Samiha sobbed.

"Listen to me," Luke began.

"We need to concentrate on what we came here to do. We need to find that Ocular even more so now than before, because we can't allow this one to fall into their hands again. If that were to happen, we'd be worse off than ever, because there is no more bargaining power."

Samiha leaned back into her seat and made an effort to stop crying. She breathed deeply several times, as she wiped the tears away from her eyes. After a minute, she seemed to regain composure and looked over at Luke.

"OK. Let's get going. Let's find that thing and get the hell out of here as soon as we can."

Luke patted her leg in a comforting gesture then started the van up. He pulled out of the observation area and continued down the narrow road to Sedona.

At the main junction in the center of town he turned east to where the roadside signs directed the way to Bell Rock. Although they had seen it before, magnified by Leo's remarkable satellite-telescope link, nothing could have prepared them for the splendor of a personal encounter.
Luke parked the van along side the road, in an area designated for sightseers and pedestrians. They left the van and approached the low fencing that kept visitors contained, and stared in wonder at the awesome majesty of Bell Rock.
This was the grandest of red rock country, where the color and natural design came together in an explosion of magnificence. The massive peak loomed high overhead in the near distance and seemed to have gone untouched for millions of years. Other unique rock creations dotted the immediate area with their own special flavor of design, but none emitted the magical attraction felt when in the presence of the Bell .

"It takes the breath away," Samiha uttered, whispering in awe. Luke studied the patterns of the weathered rock that, like layers of a cake, blended together to form a natural staircase that started at the base and continued all the way to the very summit. Most were far too wide to enable an average step, yet the groves and lines etched neatly by thousands of years of winds and rain would make it relatively easy to climb.
"We'll get some rope, a couple of nice rock hammers, and some anchor bolts to help us climb it," Luke announced.
 "Come on. Let's not waste any more time."

They drove back toward the main area of town and pulled into the first motel they came to. At the reservations desk, Luke requested a room at the rear, away from sight from the main street and where they could park their van behind the motel. Then he unpacked a few necessities while Samiha used the opportunity to take a quick shower.

Later, they walked the few blocks distance to the business district and located a hardware store, where Luke bought the items they needed. At a sporting goods shop they bought boots suitable for hiking and climbing, and outer wear that matched the color of the reddish brown terrain, with the idea to camouflage their appearance as they scaled the mount.

Once satisfied that they had everything they would need, they headed back to the motel to change into their climbing gear. Luke loaded the ropes, flashlights, and hammers into a backpack and strapped it onto himself, then they started out along the road to Bell Rock.

"We'll keep the van here," Luke decided.
"If our mercenary bastard shows up he'll probably be looking for it."
They hiked east along the main road until they came to a spot that became thick with high brush and over grown weeds, about a half-mile from the rock.
"We'll head this way," Luke directed as he stepped over the fence and helped Samhia do the same.
"This will take us around to the back side of the rock and minimize the chance of us being seen by any pain-in-the-ass bystanders or local sheriffs. It'll probably be rough going, so keep your eyes pealed for snakes and stay close to me."
"Lead the way," Samiha invited.
Although they were both very experienced climbers and hikers, and quite seasoned with precarious terrain, the going was extremely tough and the walk tiresome as they maneuvered over rocky desert ground. They hiked for another twenty minutes before they finally arrived at the back side of the massive structure.
"It's much bigger up close," Luke mentioned between gasps for air.
"They always are," Samiha agreed.

సా

At the base of the rock they rested for a while and shared some bottled water that Luke had retrieved from the backpack. He surveyed the slope carefully, looking along the side all the up to the top.

"This appears to be as good a starting point as any. You ready for this?" he asked her.

Samiha smiled at him.

"You're the one panting like a tired old hound dog."

Luke took a final sip from the water bottle before returning it to his pack, then he turned to the face of the rock and began to climb. Samiha waited until he was about fifteen feet up before she followed. As predicted, there were plenty of footholds, and adequate support that provided for a fairly easy climb, but it was still very tedious for Luke, who tired quickly. Samiha stayed with him all the way, somewhat better for wear and in much healthier condition than Luke. She scaled the surface like an old hand.

"Come on, old man," she urged him.

"Just a little further now."

When they finally reached the top Luke was exhausted, and sat down to catch his breath while Samiha stood over him, smiling and quite prepared and able to do it all over again.

"You need to exercise a little more," she told him with a laugh. Together, they relaxed for a moment to take in the view and all of the colorful surrounding landscape.

"I just thought of something," Luke announced.

"I forgot the cell phone."

Samiha shrugged her shoulders.

"What do we need it up here for?"

"I was just thinking that by now, the satellite is most likely in a position that would allow Leo to see us. And without the phone, we can't communicate with him."

Samiha raised her arm and waved at the sky.

"Well, at least he knows that we're thinking of him."

The top of Bell Rock is a smooth, flattened plateau that only spans about thirty feet in diameter, and every crack that was large enough to accommodate room for a person to pass through into its depths, was very apparent. There were four of them, all about the same size.

"Leo told us that the markings on the map ran smack dab in the middle of the rock." Luke pointed to the very center of the top, only a few feet away from where they sat.
"Right there! These others are too off to one side or the other." Samiha nodded.
"That's has to be it," she agreed.

Luke removed a fifty-foot length of the nylon rope from his backpack and began to secure it firmly by tying it around a small stationary section of jutting rock. Then he carefully knotted the rope in intervals of two feet, to allow for a good hold.
"Ok. Let's see what's in that hole," he said as he dropped the remaining length into the dark crevice.
Luke slipped into the hole and Samiha watched as he dropped down into it, and came to a landing only about ten feet from the surface.
"There's room for both us to stand," he shouted up to her.
"Then another hole veers off even deeper. Come on down." She did as he instructed and quickly shimmied down the shaft until she dropped next to him.
Their flashlights illuminated the small area that was no bigger than an average size closet, and showed another branch of the hole that began at the very end and disappeared into more darkness.
Luke sent the line down the second hole as Samiha knelt over it and shinned her light into its depths.
"Wow. That's pretty deep," she exclaimed.
"Be careful."
Luke wasted no time as he took a firm grip on the line and lowered himself slowly into the hole while Samiha looked on. She could barely make out the faint image of the bottom which was easily twenty-five to thirty feet further down.
"Take it slow and easy, Luke," she called down to him.

Luke grunted out an inaudible response as he made his way down, inch by inch pausing often to shine his light on the rocks walls around him, and the floor beneath him. After ten solid minutes of descending, he finally dropped down to the bottom.

The area was slightly larger than the closet above, and as he scanned every corner he became more and more disappointed. "There's nothing down here," he hollered to her. "This place is totally empty." Samiha didn't answer, so he yelled out to her once again. "Hey! I don't see anything down here. It's completely bare! Can you hear me?" There was a few minutes of silence, then the sound of a quick muffled thunk from above.

"Well you better look a little harder," came the shout from a man's voice that he did not recognize. The sound froze him in his boots as Luke looked up to see the grinning face of the leader of the mercenary team, who was holding Samiha's flashlight and shinning it into his own face. "Mister Ozman, how are you? We finally meet!" Luke gasped in disbelief. "Mister Ozman, if I were you, I'd start doing a bit more thorough excavation down there because you're not coming back up until you find that machine." Luke was stunned. "What have you done with Samiha?" he screamed. "You mean your girlfriend up here? Oh she's fine. Just taking a little nap. But don't you worry yourself about it. I'll take good care of her. In the meantime, you better start digging, 'cause the air down there isn't so good and you're wasting time. So get to it." "You son of a bitch!" Luke shouted in anger. "If you've harmed her..." "What are you gonna do about it?" he interrupted. "You're way down there, and I'm up here, on the good end of your only life line. Get to work. Find that machine or that's where you're gonna stay for another thousand years."

Luke's mind raced with confusion over what to do. He removed
the backpack and rummaged around through its contents until he
found one of the rock hammers. Then in sheer desperation he
dropped down to his knees and began to dig into the dirt and
sediment beneath him.

He was in a state of total despair thinking that there was
absolutely nothing that he could do, while slamming the hammer
again and again into the soft rock and dust. His thoughts raced
with fear for Samiha.

Then suddenly all hell broke loose. Loud aggressive shouts came
from above, then a series of quick gunshots rang out blasting the
narrow space with a deafening echo. Then Luke heard a man's
tortured scream as he looked up and watched in horror as the
mercenary fell head first, straight for him. Luke instinctively
grabbed the end of the hanging line from above and rushed to one
side of the tiny enclosure, just before the man plummeted through
the floor and kept going, down yet another, newly created length
of the shaft. A large gaping hole was left in his wake, and Luke
could hear the unmistakable thud of his final landing.

Then he heard Judy's voice.
"Luke are you alright?" she screamed in urgency. Luke was still
very much in shock and she had to repeat her cry again before he
answered.
"Yes. Yes, I'm ok," he muttered as he stared down the newly
created hole in the floor.
 "How is Samiha?"
"She was knocked unconscious, but there's no wound and she's
breathing. Are you sure you're ok, Luke?"
Luke struggled with a weak grin.
 "I'm fine buddy. Boy! You're a guardian angel!"
"Yeah," she replied.
 "Never mind that, just get your butt back up here."
Luke aimed his light down the long deep hole and scanned the
entire bottom.

"Hang on Judy. There's something down there besides our flying friend and I'm gonna check it out."
Judy hesitated, then called out to him again.
"Luke, be careful. That guy may still be dangerous!"
Luke moved his flashlight down into the dark pit and over the man's twisted and crumpled body, then called back up to her.
"Oh, I sincerely doubt that. Just give me a few minutes. I'm gonna climb down there and see what it is."

Luke removed another long length rope from his backpack and tied it securely to the first line, then knotted this one every two feet as he'd done with the first. Then he dropped it down into the new hole and slowly made his decent.
Once he made it to the bottom he looked down at the body of the dead man. His neck was clearly broken, but several bullet holes in his chest probably killed him before the fall.
Luke looked around was appeared to have been a well built, hidden room, buried from view by an artificial ceiling. Ancient timbers used to construct the area over head, were now in pieces at his feet from the impact of the man's fall.

Then he saw it.
Placed neatly in one corner of the small room was a large stone table and on it, an old cloth that covered a very significant shape.
He moved the cloth and it crumbled to shreds from his touch, and Luke stared in awe at what lay under it, placed there so many thousands of years before. It was another Ocular, an exact duplicate in very detail of the one he had come to know so well. Like the others, it was in pristine condition, unmarked and no signs of wear or age.

Next to it lay it's needle, and Luke smiled as he picked it up and put it in his pocket. As he picked up the machine he noticed another object that had been placed behind the Ocular. It was rectangular box made from the very same material as the Ocular, used to preserve its contents. Luke gently pried open its simple lid and stared in wonder at several rolls of ancient papyrus.

Taking care not to harm their brittle pages, he very slowly unrolled them to see a meticulously scrolled text he recognized immediately as hieroglyphics.

"They left us a memo!" he muttered to himself with a smile. He loaded his treasures into his backpack and shouted up to Judy.

"Ok. I'm coming back up!"

Several days later Luke, Samiha and Judy relaxed at the motel pool and talked as they sat under the umbrella of the outdoor table and sipped on drinks.

"Leo emailed some preliminary results of the translation on the scrolls. He says that although he and his University buddies haven't even scratched the surface of all of the content, what they have been able to translate so far is absolutely wonderful. And I agree."

He unfolded several sheets of paper and laid them out in front of him. "That's great!" Samiha exclaimed.

"Read it to us."

Luke nodded.

"Ok. But Leo advised me that they had to improvise by deciphering symbols that turned into lengthy sentences and while they felt fairly confident that the translation was accurate, it probably wasn't exactly word for word."

"Go on, read it," she urged.

Luke picked up the first of the pages and began to read it aloud to them.

"'I've written this in the language of symbols in the hope that whoever finds this will be able to understand it. Included are directions on the correct operation of the machine and my wish that its knowledge be used wisely.

"'I am a direct descendant of a group of people who escaped the disaster to our home when a devastating celestial collision occurred to our neighbor, the Great Planet. The few who made it here did so as a result of pure chance, as other survivors scattered to the moons of the Great Planet as well as other moons of the Ringed One.

"'Here, I have been able to blend in with the local natives without incident, taking special care not to disturb them or interfere with their normality. Yet I have been unable to integrate our technology without the threat of causing unwelcome attention to myself.

"'They have a very strict adherence to deeply rooted ideologies and it's very clear that their staunch beliefs restrict and even forbid the introduction of technological advancements that may be construed as the work of their *devils*. So, being only a few of a small number of our survivors, we have made the decision to bury the machines in different locations on this planet and make every attempt to choose our suggestive assistance discreetly while we settle into secret cohabitation.

"'I have found it strangely odd that the current inhabitants of this region are so intently absorbed with an unnatural attraction to the expression of negative emotions. They justify killing one another. Too many of them believe that there is not enough of the things they need to exist. They even create separations between themselves, and actually delegate specific territories to certain groups, claiming ownership and defending these areas with conflict and fierce reprisal against any who breech these borders.

"'Many are very obsessed with greed and horde goods. Some of the greedy are viewed as higher echelon in their particular tribe. They are usually the leaders, who delegate the laws and grant special considerations for residents who pay them tribute with goods or unique items of beauty. These leaders have teams of well compensated guards who keep their goods secure from harm or unauthorized sharing. They also enforce the regulations of the community as decreed by the rulers and leaders.

"'Each tribe has a different god, an imaginary supreme ruler over all, and each claims their own to be the one and true. They fester with hate for no reason and inflict harsh judgment upon others of their kind over the color of skin or other outward physical characteristics.

"Thus far I have not encountered a single native who has the slightest inkling of their innate power to develop objective consciousness. They are completely unaware of their universal bond. They know nothing of the vast universal energy that connects every being. They are blinded by their daily needs and obsessions and never stop to search within for their real worth.

"'I know that in time, with the natural course of evolution, these beliefs of theirs will gradually dissipate and change. They always do. But for now, they continue to drain the energy of their beings with negative emotions and stifle their true spiritual growth. They wallow in the beliefs handed down from peers, teachers and parents and justify emotions like fear, guilt, regret, anger, disgust, vengeance, hatred, jealously, feelings of inferiority and superiority and all degrees of the same.

"'Yet I see the gentle side. I see them as for what they are, my brothers and sisters, still very young and inexperienced. I see them as the beings *we* once were, with a long road of spiritual development before them.

"'Our message to you is simple.
"'The universe is permeated with human intelligence, some of us farther along the path of evolution than others, yet identical in being and origin. Circumstances beyond our control have brought us together here in this new land, with new acquaintances, and presented the opportunity to help. I will mingle with you, and I will try my best to help you in any way I can.'"

Luke placed the notes down and looked at the awe struck expressions on the faces of his two friends and he smiled at them.
"What do you think?" he asked them.
Judy was shaking her head in utter disbelief.
"Absolutely mind boggling!" she proclaimed.
"Unbelievable!" Samiha agreed, and she continued,
"If I didn't know better I'd say that the person who wrote that was related to you, Luke."

Luke grinned.

"Listen to you," he added with a chuckle.

"The fact of the matter is, that *I am* related, and so are you. Don't you see? This was written at a time when the population of the Earth didn't even total of all of the people in Chicago . It's likely that most of the people on the entire planet are also related to him or one of others in the group of survivors."

"You mean that these survivors probably mated with the locals?" Judy asked.

"Of course!" Luke responded with unwavering conviction, and he continued,

"And why wouldn't they? Their home was gone now, destroyed or at least rendered uninhabitable because of the collision. They knew all of this and probably long before it actually happened."

"It all makes a lot of sense now," Judy remarked.

Samiha remained silent for a long time, dwelling reverently over the words Luke had just narrated, and obviously stuck with new insight and possibilities.

"So what do we do now?" she asked.

Luke leaned toward her and kissed her lips passionately before replying.

"We enjoy our vacation for another week or so and go back home. We have a lot of work to do, a lot of new things to learn of the real history of the Earth and the universe as we know it.

"I'm anxious to see what other wonders those ancient scrolls have to say." She smiled lovingly at him and turned her attention to Judy.

"What about you, Judy?" She asked. What will you do?"

Judy shrugged her shoulders.

"I have no plans. I was kinda hoping to hang around with you."

అ